Days
of
Light

Days
of
Light

A novel

MEGAN HUNTER

Grove Press
New York

First published in Great Britain in 2025 by Picador,
an imprint of Pan Macmillan

Printed in the United States of America

First Grove Atlantic hardcover edition: June 2025

ISBN 978-0-8021-6477-3
eISBN 978-0-8021-6478-0

Library of Congress Cataloging-in-Publication data is available for this title.

Grove Press
an imprint of Grove Atlantic
154 West 14th Street
New York, NY 10011

Distributed by Publishers Group West

groveatlantic.com

25 26 27 28   10 9 8 7 6 5 4 3 2 1

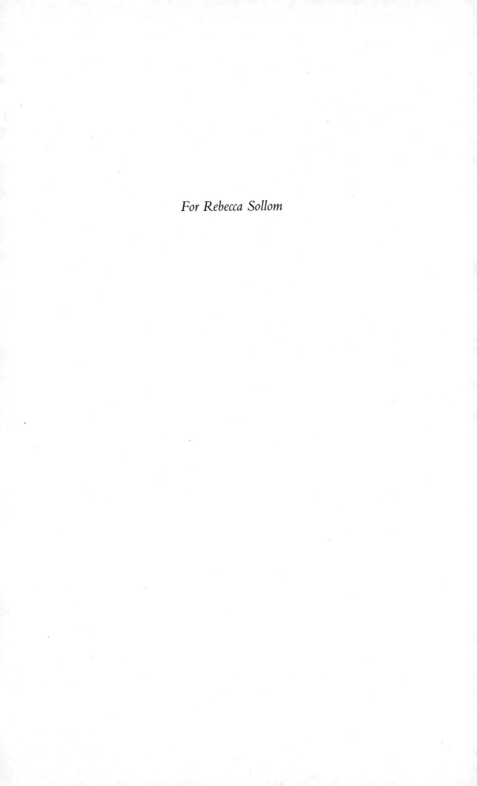

For Rebecca Sollom

And the light shineth in darkness; and the darkness
comprehended it not.
The Gospel of John 1:5

What is all this juice and all this joy?
Gerard Manley Hopkins, 'Spring'

DAY ONE

Easter Sunday 1938

WHEN IVY LOOKED back, this was what she remembered.

Joseph was singing. Here was a rare thing her brother couldn't do: his voice was tuneless, rambling, reaching for a note as though for a high ledge on a mountain. But the fact remained: Joseph – their own plain, sensible Joseph – was singing. He lay in his bed in the next room, the painted walls sentinel around him, his window ajar, already wafting sweetness. He was opening his wide lips, feeling the vibration build in his stomach, rise into his chest. Here was music: in his throat, on his tongue, whistling through his teeth. Ivy held her own breath, to try to hear the song more clearly. It was a low, almost continuous sound, a bird on a summer night; an anonymous, homeless tone, the sound of yearning itself.

Ivy pictured Joseph in his set at Oxford, the two little rooms with their air of adolescent disarray, his girlfriend a shape at the edges. Their father, Gilbert, had given him a gramophone for his twenty-first birthday, and surely Joseph would dance his girl around the study, taking care not to bump into the clumsy armchairs, the solemn wooden desk.

Joseph was a good dancer; he would have his arm wrapped around her waist. Ivy could see the waist – its deep dip of invitation, its stretch into arm and shoulder – but above this was a blur. Joseph had never described this girl much beyond her name – *Frances* – and just once, after dinner and wine: *lovely*.

Over time, Ivy had filled this blur with figures: a girl leaning to pick up a penny, rising like a child who has stamped her gumboots into a puddle, with a loose, opening smile. Or: a more serious woman, wearing a beret at an angle, a cigarette tucked between her fingers, lips poised with experience. Sometimes, the figure was simple, even incestuous: herself, or her mother. Ivy did not berate herself for this; after all, after today, these figures would vanish for ever. Today, the real Frances would visit for Easter.

Through her open window Ivy could smell the goodness of the garden outside, the truth of another morning arriving. The birds made their expectant, nervous morning calls; even they knew about this day, Ivy felt. They sensed its particular quality, how even at Cressingdon – *the most secular house in England*, Mother had once called it – Easter meant something. It meant something to the trees, and to the greying statues of the garden, their subtle turns only children could see. When Ivy was six or seven she had watched the small nymph by the pond turn and wink at her. It was, perhaps, the single most significant moment of her childhood – magic proven, the shell of reality cracked. But when she tugged, hard, on her mother's skirts, Marina only said *of course, darling*, and moved away.

Ivy heard a noise from the kitchen below her; Anne would have been up for hours, taking the lamb from the larder, covering it with salt and herbs, hoping to disguise the way the air had already dried the meat a little. It would be a warm Easter, the newspapers said, using that word *unseasonable*, but wasn't Easter always sunny? Ivy closed her eyes, felt a threaded seam of past Easter Sundays: those when they had eaten in the drawing room, and in the garden room, and in the garden itself. An image of sunlight through a tablecloth: she must have sat under the table, as a child, been passed morsels of meat by Joseph or Angus, her head patted like a dog. The sunlight seemed thinner, in memory, a different colour even, more lemon, lighter than the dense peach that hung around her now. She turned on her back, lifted her nightdress over her head and breathed her own morning smell: she was like a farm, she often thought, so many parts working together to create the semblance of order, one shape moving through the world.

The singing had stopped, but there was another noise from Joseph's room now, a clunk and a creak, as though he had left his bed and then thought better of it, turned back against the cool gravity of the painted wall. Sometimes in the night she heard him snoring, a steady whinny that reminded her of a horse, the way breath came warm through their deep nostrils, their long, patient exhalations. She was usually up before Joseph, but she wondered now if he had woken even earlier than she had, enjoying the quiet of himself, the smell of the garden rising towards him.

But here; the singing began again. There was something unformed and tender in his voice, a tone she had not heard since his childhood, in his offerings of worms or mud pies, the sudden wail of his disagreement at the dinner table. She thought of his hair, as it used to be, the monkish circle of brown that often fell in his eyes. He was always bigger than Ivy, always two years ahead, but now she remembered him coltish, fawn-like; she remembered the soft skin of his arms, the tangle of his legs on the privy when he left the door open. And now: now he was in love, the prospect of love still more potent in the face of likely war, Joseph their *golden boy*, the only son.

This vacation Ivy had looked for love on her brother. Not only looked: she *felt* for it, when she thought he might not notice, resting her hand casually on his scalp or forearm until he batted it away. She thought she might feel love in his skin, that it might give his hairy arms or bony knees some new softness, a feminine grace. She had wondered, even before he arrived, if he would smell different, if his voice would fall in a different key. And now, here it was at last, the clear signal, not a sight or a touch but a sound, after all. He was singing.

★

Her feet were bare: the grass on her skin was a blanket of kisses. This was the phrase she thought of, *blanket of kisses*, imagining each wet press of the lawn as a wide mouth opening on her heels, the soft pads beneath her toes. She had been trying to write poetry lately, had been trying to content herself with being unkissed, untouched, to imagine that nature itself was her lover, that the whole world – meaning nobody – could adore her. She sat down on the old swing in the little apple orchard, though she knew the damp seat would leave marks. She liked the feel of wood against her skin, the secret regard that was so much like the esteem she held for herself, in the bath, when no one was looking, the gentle approval she felt for her breasts, her thighs, the dip of her elbow. This wood held her, she felt. It knew her. She pushed herself off, her feet moving into the mud.

From here Ivy could see the whole house, its back turned towards her, something modest, almost shy, about the square hulking of each upper window. She knew only Joseph was up there now, still somehow in bed, an hour after she had heard him singing. Angus would be in the studio he shared with Marina, hidden behind the curve of the house, his brush in his mouth or his fingers. Easter would mean little to him, perhaps the least of them all; a slightly larger lunch, more people in the house to distract and unmoor him. He was to be a great painter, it was said. Perhaps he already was.

There would be Marina's sister, Genevieve, and her husband, Hector, both writers – she a novelist, he a sometime

7

playwright – down the road from their own country cottage. They would ask Angus about his art, and he would evade them, with a dip of his head, a slight pursing of the mouth. This had always amazed Ivy: how people would let Angus simply not answer a question, how he could create a bubble of silence and bounce it, casually, in the air above the table.

Gilbert would be here too, the father who was soft in body and sharp in mind, so ramshackle in his appearance that he had once been mistaken – in the British Library no less – for a tramp. Once, Ivy had asked Marina if they would ever divorce, and her mother had put her cup down – they were taking tea in the garden. She stared, her face fixed, as though her daughter had said something obscene. This despite the fact that Gilbert lived with Dorothy now, and before that Ursula, and Maud before her. But it was true, at least, that these women never came to Cressingdon. Gilbert was driving down with Bear, Marina had said – their old friend Rupert, named partly for his slight stoop, his way of walking as though about to pull the world into his arms. Ivy pictured the two of them in the car, like inverse images of manhood; Gilbert slack and pallid, Bear smooth and solid as bronze.

At breakfast, Marina had been eating; this was a good sign. Looking at her plate was like looking at the sky in the morning, a forecast of whether things would be fair and settled, or if a storm was coming, not yet visible on the horizon. Marina had eaten a piece of bread today, spread thickly with butter, a glaze of jam across it. This was the best that could be hoped for, even if she would never eat it all. One summer, she had all but given up food, retreated to the studio to paint for days at a time, only leaving to use the privy or sip water. Later, Angus told Ivy that her mother had eaten when they were all asleep: *water biscuits*, he said. *Pears.* For Marina, food and art were incompatible in some way, just as religion and art were, and even politics and art to a certain degree. The borders of art needed to be policed, it seemed, kept safe from intruders of the body and mind. When Marina ate – or put food on her plate – it meant she consented to be in the world, to join her family in life, at least for the day.

Now there was a movement at the middle upper window, so sudden it felt joyful, a brisk jolt of the curtains that seemed strong enough to tear them, and there was Joseph, not yet dressed, his wide pale chest a boyish version of Gilbert's. His head bent as he spotted Ivy on the swing, and the window opened – it opened! Ivy could feel the film of solitude broken, something livelier entering the morning at last.

Ive! What're you doing?

She shrugged on the swing, made a self-mocking grimace.

Nothing!

When was she ever doing anything? It seemed aeons since she'd been at school, though it had barely been a year. Since then: a dozen careers considered, at least. Dancer, painter, singer. When she was feeling more noble: nurse, adventurer. Spy.

Joseph burst from the kitchen doors, a shirt slung around his shoulders but not buttoned, a hunk of bread in his hand. Why was it, Ivy wondered, that his hands themselves seemed to have become bread, to have the exact texture and colour of what he held? She had noticed this before, how her brother merged with whatever surrounded him, an easeful camouflage. And there was something in the sheer sturdiness of his fingers – so round, with their stub nails – that made her think of dough, of shaping it with Anne on long dull afternoons, the kitchen windows blinded by rain.

The sun moved from behind a cloud, and Joseph positioned himself in the smoothest patch of grass beside her. His clothes would dampen, but she knew he wouldn't care. *They'll dry*, he would say with a shrug. Joseph trusted the processes of the earth – the inevitable turning of the world, the passage of the sun – in a way Ivy had never been able to. When they were small Ivy would have nightmares about the failure of reality – the sky falling down, the ocean grown large and dark as a shroud – and she would creep across the whining floorboards of the passage to Joseph's bedroom, to hug against his large, pulsing back. Their mother had found them in the morning the last time this had happened; she proclaimed that Ivy was *far too old* for it. Ivy could still feel the cool of Marina's hands as she reached under the blankets to separate them, unpeeling one child from the other.

Happy Easter, Joseph murmured now, his eyes closed, the dappled shadow of the trees tickling his lips, his eyelids. He was the first to say it to her, and he seemed to make the day what it was, in a way Anne's cooking or the calling birds could not. In the manner of siblings they were always children when they were together, could never fully step into their adult forms, rise to their true heights. Ivy wondered for a second if Joseph would hide chocolate eggs about the garden, as he used to. But then she remembered: he would have so much else to think about.

Are you looking forward to Frances coming?

It was a stupid question, she knew, and she pushed herself off again on the swing to conceal her awkwardness, the branches of the apple tree creaking above her. She loved the way the air came to meet her, a soft wind, an invisible lifting.

Hmm. To her surprise, Joseph seemed to be considering this question. *Bit nervous about her meeting Mater if I'm honest — and the rest.*

It had always been something delicate, the question of how to explain their family to those outside it, whether to be proud or ashamed. *It's a new way of living*, Ivy had attempted to tell her classmates. When she was met with embarrassed silence, or, once, a kind of guffaw, she found herself returning to the old smudged terms: their mother lived with her *friend*, Angus, father had to live in London for work.

I've told her — everything, Joseph said now. *She's very understanding.*

Ivy leant back, let her hair touch the grass behind her, feeling gravity tip her body into the earth, only lightly held by the thin panel of the swing. She felt pained for Joseph, as though she was responsible for their parents' arrangements, the complicated offering he had to make to Frances, his first ever girlfriend. Or at least *the only one we know about*, as Marina had said, making Ivy imagine a murky late-night Oxford, Joseph as a shadowed figure in a panama hat, kissing women in doorways. The thought had made her smile; she knew Joseph would do no such thing. But could she herself be kissed in doorways? she wondered. There had only been two kisses in her life – she touched her lips now, as though for evidence, lifting one hand from the rope of the swing – and both had been appalling; wet messes that made her doubt not only kissing but life itself, the promises that had been made for it.

She gripped the ropes of the swing: they were starting to burn her hands, but it was not unpleasant. Was kissing – and all its expansions – not the height of experience, according to those who had lived? And what had it been, for Ivy? A cruel pressing of one body (one farm!) into another, a night-marish sensation of attempted contact. Why, she had wondered, was this regarded as connection? A stranger's tongue against her own, his hand beginning to rummage in her blouse. *It meant nothing to her*: she had heard this phrase somewhere, and it was almost adequate. But the kisses had been more than nothing: they had been disasters, and still more than this: they were proof that she was alone in some crucial way, that she could not be reached by touch. But her brother could be, it seemed. He had chosen someone, written about her in letters home since Michaelmas term, only brief ones to Ivy but such long essays to Marina, each with more flourishes than the last. Their mother had taken to reading them aloud with her morning coffee, her glasses perched on the very end of her nose.

She's the daughter of a clergyman, Angus! Can you imagine?

Very holy-moly, Angus had said, eyebrows raised, taking a large bite of toast. Ivy envied his detachment from Joseph's affairs; she would have loved to have felt indifferent to Joseph in any way, but most of all in this: her brother's success in *finding someone,* when she had been such a resolute failure. And perhaps this was what gave Angus his relaxed disposition: his sheer confidence, the arch of his shoulder blade so long and silent, so entirely itself and for himself. He was Marina's, people assumed, but he was so much more than this: he was his own.

Joseph threw the head of a daisy at her. He was sitting up now, she saw, crossing his legs like the Buddha statue in the studio, his stomach a soft lip at the edge of his waistband.

Wake up, dreamy head! You're going to fall off that swing.

The wood had begun to irritate her legs, even through the cotton of her nightdress. Ivy lifted herself from the swing, feeling heavy, and lay down next to Joseph, her thighs soothed by the cool grass, dampness already spreading across her back. There would be grass stains, she realized, and Anne would scrub them, her face puce over the washtub. Ivy could not bring herself to feel guilt; she felt little of anything, lying like an animal on the earth. People had so many sophistications, but wasn't this the greatest pleasure of all? To be soothed by simple life: body, sun, her heart's sustaining rhythm within her.

Looking forward to seeing Bear then?

He had turned towards her, his smile the perfect line of her own embarrassment, the sun glancing lightly on his cheek; he had no problems, she saw, it was only she who was a tangle of feeling, who harboured these knots of shame. She let the feelings go, felt the contact of her heel against her brother's shin, hard.

Ow! That's a bit much, Ive. I'm only joshing.

You promised.

Her lower lip was jutting out, she knew. She wanted to cross her arms but knew it would look ridiculous, lying on her back. A warm tear began to roll down her cheek.

Oh, Ive. Don't—

Joseph was sitting up now, pushing his hair back with his hands, always a sign he was uncomfortable.

I don't like him any more, I told you that.

Her mouth had become small, her words staccato with childishness. She felt she was watching herself as though in a cinema. Was that girl – messy hair, damp nightdress – telling the truth? She thought of Bear, of the last time she saw him:

an earlier, cooler spring day, a movement of his fairness, the turn of his cheek. His narrowed look into the distance, as though searching for a rare bird. She tried to steady him in her mind, now, to find a single image, floating as though in water; he was a merman, now, shirtless. She could imagine his tail, the scales of it, the way it rose up and down as he swam. She smirked, despite herself.

Well, good. He's a bit old for you – to say the least.

It was true that Bear was a man, not mythical after all but of the same generation as her parents. What did Marina say on his last birthday? Forty-four, some neat symmetry. And then there was she: nineteen, and looking even younger, people often said. *A baby.*

Joseph turned a thick blade of grass over his fingers, lifted it to his mouth and lowered it again.

He gave me his book, you know. Pretty saucy. Fancy it?

Ivy shook her head, pursed her mouth dismissively, though she would have loved to see just one page. She put her hand to her eyes as the sun moved behind a rare cloud, the whole garden changing in an instant, cloaked in shadow. She was beginning to feel that Easter would not be the feast she had imagined, that the day was not as porous as it had seemed, just hours ago. The whole place did not know its particular joy after all. She longed to have a feeling that persisted for more than a week, for more than an hour, even. But the world was constantly changing and moving, becoming itself. Joseph lay down again: he turned his face to her.

You'll fall in love one day, Ivy, I promise. It's the most—

He breathed out, just like his snoring, a gust of gentle patience.

It's the most spectacular thing in the world.

By late morning she was expected; expected to help, to be present, to be dressed in something that spoke of springtime, the bursting forth of new life. She chose her yellow linen smock, not quite smart enough but surely in keeping with the day, and a wide-brimmed straw hat that Joseph said made her look like a scarecrow. She felt a jumble of limbs in fabric, a person unformed, unable to present herself to the world. When she came downstairs Marina only narrowed her eyes briefly before nodding, as though in dismissal. Perhaps, Ivy thought, even Marina was trying to lift herself to the occasion: her whole family was coming to lunch. Her son was in love. It was Easter Day – flowers would be arranged. The sun would shine on them all. Today, just today, they would not speak of war, or government planning. They would not even speak of the war in Spain. There would be no grand conflict: they would trust the blueness of the sky, for once, the ripe greenness of the grass.

It was Ivy's job to pick the flowers; Marina had only to motion to the empty vases on the table in the drawing room, each setting laid and expectant, the tablecloth freshly washed. Ivy welcomed the chance to leave the house again, the tense, humid atmosphere created by cooking meat, the brief words of Anne and Marina as they made their preparations. She felt the mildness of the air mould itself to her as she moved through the garden, finding each small curve of her body, knowing it as no one else had.

The flowers were only clutches of daffodils, growing in nodding bunches in the tiny wood behind the orchard. Ivy crouched in her sandals, gripping stalk after stalk, feeling the break of their fluted throats in her fingers. She liked the smell they gave her hands: a yeasted, slightly metallic moisture. Sometimes she felt that she would have preferred to live as a flower, or a tree, to grow in increments, never be expected to move or create beyond her natural cycle. It was statements like this that made her teachers roll their eyes. *So dramatic*, they said of her. Or simply: *peculiar*. When she'd first arrived at the school they had expected her to be extraordinary, coming from the family she did, the daughter of artists – famous ones, at that. But when she displayed no outstanding talents, to their surprise, they seemed to hope only for ordinariness, for her to be just like the others. Girls with no talents should be good at sports, it seemed, or at least *jolly*, or *kind*, or some other helpful quality. Girls with no talents had no right to be philosophical, or morbid. They should not hope to be trees.

Inside, Ivy arranged the flowers in jugs on the long table in the garden room. She stood back in appreciation, as she had seen Marina do, taking in the room as though it were a stage set, the table's silverware winking, the walls glowing with warm light, each daffodil seeming held, forgiven. From the front of the house came the rumble of a car, clear and human as an approaching voice.

They're here! Ivy, go and fetch Angus!

Marina never wanted to greet guests alone; she liked to stand with Angus at the front of the house, like figures in an architect's model, never to present herself as solitary, even for a moment. But Angus would not take part in the fripperies of flower arranging and place setting. He would not lean over Anne's shoulder, as Marina did, and ask that she add lemon juice to the gravy, or extra herbs to the lamb. He could not take part in the atmosphere of waiting. Instead, he would stay in the studio until the last possible moment, just as Gilbert had stayed in his office before him. It was this, Ivy knew, that produced the desperation in Marina's voice, the sense that the sound had been stretched to its breaking point.

Ivy left by the outer doors, took the few steps in her bare feet to the entrance of the studio. The grass was warming now, only a memory of its morning dampness close to the soil. As she approached the door she heard music from the gramophone; a hushed concerto, a small team of violins. She could smell the studio already: a mix of turpentine and exertion, smoke and the faintest trace of lamb from the house, threaded through its art like a reminder of animal life, of the need to eat.

Angus? They're here now – someone's here, anyway—

Angus wore a painting shirt and old trousers, Ivy saw: he was not dressed for lunch. He stood, unmoving, in front of his canvas, his brush held in mid-air. How, Ivy wondered for the thousandth time, did he know how to be an artist? She did not understand how he pretended not to have heard her, or truly did not hear her, so immersed was he in the moment of creation. When she tried to paint, or write, she was constantly distracted, by anything at all: a fly, an interesting bird glimpsed from the window, a memory or thought, the slightest pang of hunger or fatigue or excitement. And yet here was Angus, not turning at all.

He raised his brush: Ivy had the exhilarating sense, for a moment, that she did not exist, or at least was invisible, that she could watch him as long as she wanted. He made a dabbing mark, his elbow moving only very slightly, its impression hidden from Ivy. She turned her head so she could see more clearly. A thin blue deepening into darker blue: a section of sky.

Angus? Ivy?

It was Marina's *guests* voice, audible even from inside the house, something unmistakably desperate coursing through its politeness. Angus looked up, a hand rising to his face.

Oh, the blasted lunch.

Perhaps, Ivy thought, he was speaking to himself. But as he turned she realized he had known she was there; he had simply kept himself in his painting, just as he wanted to. His ability to do this had perhaps been present at his birth, Ivy thought, passed on by the focus of his military father. Even as an infant he was probably extraordinary. But she still felt it was possible that she might change, as a caterpillar becomes a moth, that she could wake up one morning and find herself a true artist, saved from distraction.

Angus's face, as he turned, was almost bashful, something boyish around his eyes and mouth.

We'd better go in, hadn't we?

Ivy nodded. She would have liked to sit on the chaise longue and watch him paint a little longer, she realized. She was not ready for the lunch, with its conversation formalized as a script, its shifting allegiances and moods. She felt – moving with Angus through the hush of the studio, out into the brightness of the garden – that only Frances could make the meal something new, could transform its stiffness into the free-flowing pleasure of a party. She thought of her flowers, as though each were a different Frances she had never met, each with a certain dimension of a woman, one bowing, the other lifting her head.

The lamb was overcooked. It was eaten apologetically, with masses of gravy, knives and forks scraping back and forth on the best plates. Marina had changed the positions of the jugs, Ivy saw, moving each one a little to the left or right. Ivy resisted the urge to reach out – to place her arms over all of the guests – and move them back. They had arrived almost simultaneously, the two cars carrying Gilbert and Bear, Genevieve and Hector; Ivy could picture Gilbert's stately Wolseley standing sentry beside Genevieve's sleek convertible in the drive. Marina was in the midst of them when Ivy and Angus came in from the studio, her arms raised as though she was drowning.

Angus! Our guests!

Anne? The wine?

She hated having company; this was the truth of it. Ivy had seen how exhausted she was after dinners and parties, dried and weak, as though every drop of moisture had been taken from her. But still she invited them; still she smiled and turned and hugged and kissed. Ivy had learnt how to do this from her mother; she had been just as convincing, raising her voice to a high song of welcome, opening her arms as though her body was not her own, as though anyone could touch it. And they did touch her, Aunt Genevieve pulling her close for one of those strangely intimate kisses, her breath warm and spiced, Ivy's lips touching her papery cheek, Uncle Hector's hand carefully on her shoulder. But it was only Bear who wrapped a hand around her waist, a hand that Ivy found herself noticing despite herself, its tanned fingers covered in hair. What did it feel like, she wondered, to have such a hand? To place it on the leg of your trousers, as Bear did after he touched her, and then to move it through your hair? Bear had the hair of a matinee idol, Marina always said. It fell in exactly the right place. Watching him, Ivy felt how much easier it would be to be a man, to place yourself exactly as you intended, for your body and mind to be one entity, controlled by the same force. She shifted on her chair, chewing the same piece of lamb over and over, her teeth failing her. She lifted her napkin to her mouth. Across the table, Bear ate with the speed and relish of a person starved, the meat no obstacle, gravy dripping from his fork. Even Joseph eyed him across the table, as he took his own steady mouthfuls, his eyes full of a question. From one head of the table, Marina kept the conversation afloat.

Did you see the notice for Angus's show? I know he's far too modest to mention it but I—

From the other end, Angus smiled but said nothing: he added salt to his food.

Absolutely splendid, Genevieve said. *Not that we would have had any doubts—*

Only a small gallery, Marina said. *But such a dear little room . . .*

There was no reply to this for a few seconds; Ivy felt the danger in these moments, the exposure of something sulphurous threatening to seep through the cracks of the afternoon. It was Joseph who closed the gap, who knew to speak before the silence gathered to its full meaning.

Magnificent, wasn't it. He said this looking at his lunch, but with such simple finality that the whole room seemed to relax. Joseph was bright, but uncomplicated: that was the family understanding. The rest of them could only look to him, as they looked to the sun, close their eyes to his blessing. The fact that he could still play this role, even today, seemed to speak still more to its truthfulness, to his strength among them.

Next to Joseph, a blank plate shone, as though it had never been sullied by food or soap, as though it had been made just today, as a work of art instead of a utensil, its virgin white the brightest thing in the room. It made a good substitute for Frances, Ivy thought, this person she had never met, who had begun to appear as a clear, knowing lightness in her mind. The absence had been barely remarked upon so far, Marina perhaps sensing that Joseph would not permit fussing over its details.

She must have missed the train—

He had said this once, and then a few minutes later:

The trains are abysmal on Sundays. And a holiday no less!

She had insisted that she would walk from the station, Joseph had told them only yesterday, and these words – *she insists on walking* – had filled Ivy with a mysterious joy, a sense that life was wider than she imagined it, filled with greater promise than she had dared to hope for. At this moment, Frances had legs to walk with, hair that streamed as she crossed the field, *insisting* on it. Knowing it was what she wanted.

But there had been no knock at the door: there was no scented young woman sitting next to Joseph, carefully cutting at the tough meat. Every utterance seemed designed to move around this absence, to avoid its edges.

Bear, the book is finished now, yes?

This from Genevieve, herself the author of several novels, a writer who seemed to Ivy to write much as a silkworm makes silk: as an expression of her nature. Ivy knew her aunt could not understand Bear's tortured process, his piles of incomplete books, unfollowed ideas and – even worse – the books finished and left for dead. Genevieve's own creation was not without complication, but it was always achieved, resolved. Ivy felt the beginnings of sympathy for Bear, together with a flaring of irritation at Genevieve. What, exactly, was she asking?

But it was Joseph, once again, who redeemed them, only a trace of weariness audible under his enthusiasm.

Fantastic stuff, Bear, really. I haven't quite finished but—

Was this all that was required, after all? Simple words of confidence? *Fantastic. Magnificent.* What would happen, Ivy wondered, if she attempted the same thing? She would be laughed at, she suspected. Or if not laughed at, then tolerated. There was no chance of her holding together the lunch as Joseph did, placing his knife and fork carefully on his plate. It was only Joseph, it seemed that day, who knew how to live. Angus and Marina could paint, and Genevieve and Bear and Gilbert and Hector could write, but none of them could live, and Ivy could do nothing, and still she could not live. She thought of slipping under the table, as she had as a child. Would this be tolerated? Would they not all be relieved, in a sense, to have a child in the family again? She had felt, when they were younger, the way that childhood rescued her family from its contradictions, its tensions, the rampant perusal of art above all else. When there was a child present, people could not behave however they wished. There was a person to be fed, and read to, and influenced. There was to be a continuation of life, and not only of art.

But Ivy did not go under the table. She had felt there, every few minutes, the nudge of Bear's foot against her own, never with quite enough firmness or consistency to rule out accidental contact. Whenever she looked up, his face was fixed in its polite tilting, his food long finished, his chin resting informally on his hand. *Too handsome for his own good*, Marina had described him, and Ivy wondered what this could possibly mean. Perhaps, she thought, he seduced too many people, or was seduced, or perhaps – this seemed more likely – he allowed his handsomeness to interfere with his novels, so that life obstructed his art. If he were uglier, perhaps he would be more widely published.

By the time Anne came in with the pudding, the lunch already felt like a failure. They all knew it, the room seemed heavy with it, and Anne seemed to lower the treacle tart with a feeling of gradual resignation. As a child, Ivy would have believed in the transformative power of Anne's treacle tart, in a situation like this, would have felt that it could in some way replace Frances herself, the sweetness and pastry almost love in the mouth. But now she knew that food did not have that power, was too fleeting to be reality itself. With her last bite, she felt Bear's foot again: unmistakable this time, a longer press, and when she lifted her eyes he was smiling, as though he knew something she did not.

After lunch the party retired to a shady table in the garden for coffee, Angus twirling his spoon in his cup, his gaze flicking up every few minutes to the glass doors of the studio. Soon, Ivy knew, he would slide from the group as though it was nothing, stroll towards his paintings as though he could not feel Marina's gaze on his back, her twitching endurance of company, her own swallowed desire to paint.

In the quiet, the cups quivered: their colours were unchanged by the silence. They had been the same cups since Ivy was born, since her mother was born: at their edges, tiny chips from other occasions in the garden, careless moments, sudden laughter. Marina poured the coffee, but it seemed cold as soon as it left the pot.

Bear had taken a deckchair, the only one of them who looked relaxed, his legs sloping into the grass, a linen hat propped low on his face. Joseph, Ivy saw, was biting his nails. Here were the nerves beneath the solidity, the last glimpses of the little boy who used to cry over dying stars during Gilbert's summer talks on astronomy, asking why they could not last for ever. She remembered the way his face had looked then: beseeching, as though their father could change the facts of the universe.

As Angus's gaze moved to the studio, Ivy saw her brother's eyes drawn again and again to the gate, which at any moment could move, open, restore the day at last. But it remained closed. The coffee was drunk. Hector and Marina had begun to discuss Chamberlain's latest speech.

Ivy had known so many other family days to end in disarray, the furniture of their relations upended, the very ceilings themselves seeming dulled and fragile, liable to collapse. There had been the day – almost mythical now, a symbol of itself – when Gilbert left, and somehow a dinner was called to mark it. It was not clear whose idea this was, or what possible good it could do. But pork was roasted with apples. There was a good Bordeaux. And Ivy had felt herself melting: dipping into the carpet, slowly lessening until she feared there would be nothing left of her. She remembered Gilbert's face that day, saw how little of that pale fear remained, now that he was loved and fed elsewhere.

Now, her father sat above his coffee, not speaking much, but gazing into his son's face with a gentle, mottled sympathy. He had been looking forward to meeting Frances, Ivy knew; he loved women. Or: he appreciated them. He viewed and absorbed them. He lived at their margins, and was shaded by their colours. He understood something about them, Ivy felt, some sloping softness, a graduated path of understanding. And yet Ivy did not feel that he had ever known her, had ever even had a single sharp breath of understanding his own daughter.

Perhaps, she considered, this was because she was not a woman, as other women were. Ivy had the sense, as a child, that her soul was not quite womanly. But Gilbert had surely not seen this. He did not know how she had dreamt, as a child of eight or nine, of sailing around the world, boyishly, in a sloop or a sunfish, her face bared to the wind and waves. Or of her thousand other imaginations, few of them feminine. But the fact remained: he could only face her as a girl, not a woman. A girl was something Gilbert – having just a brother, attending school with only boys – did not know, could not even begin to learn, it seemed. Ivy lifted her cup to her mouth, drank her coffee cold.

It was in a moment of nothing: this is how all things begin. The dark wood of the chair creaked, the swing bowed empty in the breeze. Somewhere, a bird turned in the sky. Another called to it. Was this not every moment of Easter Sunday, filled with a greeting that was barely itself? And yet this was the moment: the gathering moan of the gate, the sun behind a cloud and in the next moment shining, the gate open now, and a figure there, definitely there: a woman in green, so that at first Ivy saw nothing but face, and hands, and hair. Frances.

When Joseph stood his chair fell back: this was perfect. It

was the sound they had all been waiting for, more than this: expecting, even praying for, if they had been the types to pray. It was the afternoon breaking, gloriously, loosing form after all, fragmenting into joy. Into her.

Ivy did not know how Frances did it: ate with them all staring, so that she took in not only food but gaze after gaze, so many eyes and expressions, Gilbert's furrowed brow, Genevieve's flashing enthusiasm. But she did eat: she ate every part of Anne's meal, never getting gravy around her mouth as Ivy did, or gulping water, but swallowing a single mouthful followed by a delicate sip. It had seemed polite, to gather around the dining table again, to re-enact the meal, in some small way, with Frances now instated. She made eating look as though it could be a civilized thing to do in public, a new, dignified act. It seemed that Joseph had found someone else who could live, who understood humanity not as some happenstance or mistake but a full, bold flowering of existence.

It had been the trains, she had reassured them all, an explanation that needed no prolongment, though Gilbert had been the one to ask for details, which she gave seamlessly between bites, Joseph nodding in agreement as though he too had been there.

We simply stopped in a field! For at least an hour. The guard said there was a cow on the line.

They had all laughed, but Ivy saw that Joseph only smiled,

his eyes shining. He was, perhaps, imagining Frances in the sun-filled carriage, her suitcase on the rack above her, her legs crossed neatly, steam still billowing past the windows. He could be thinking, as Ivy herself did, of how she looked out of the window, imagining the unseen house, the unseen family, the whole unspent day spread before her.

When Frances finished, Genevieve begged tiredness: she had a long day tomorrow, she said, while Hector stood by her side in mute agreement. Ivy pictured the *long day*: five hours of writing followed by a brisk walk in the fields, perhaps a nap before a restorative supper. *Very long indeed*, Marina said predictably when her sister had gone, lifting her eyes to the ceiling.

After they were waved goodbye it did not seem possible to go back into the garden, to more coffee, the meandering drift of conversation. These things were over, they all seemed to know, perhaps for ever, with the arrival of late afternoon, of Frances herself. Neither did Angus go to the studio. Instead, he conjured a bottle of brandy, and the crystal glasses Marina kept on the highest shelf. In the drawing room, Bear put on the gramophone: a slow saxophone crept along each piece of furniture, each rise and fall of the room beginning to burn with the touch of the music.

With a single sip of brandy, Ivy felt the evening being born. Here was Frances, in her brother's arms, their touch cautious but full of intention, his head thrown back, laughing, as they danced. She had never seen Joseph like this: his being flooding his face, his skin so porous that every light of personality poured from it, fell like a visible mark on Frances, her own smile shy but complete.

At first, Ivy sat at the edge, as Marina and Gilbert did, the sofa soft with defeat, the small dance floor of the drawing-room rug lit from a single bulb overhead. Angus and Bear danced side by side, hips shifting, graceful as young boys. Angus reached a hand for Marina and she lifted herself slowly, stiff with reluctance before relaxing into her own shape, her pale hands circled around Angus's waist. Ivy looked away, watched Frances's every movement instead: her fingers on Joseph's shirt, feet moving from side to side, her dress swaying over them, a naturalness in her form like Bear's, as though she was exactly as she supposed herself to be.

Next to Ivy, Gilbert turned with a shrug.

The last ones standing – or sitting, I suppose.

He laughed at his own joke, rearranged his legs. He gestured to the rug, the people lifting and falling in the half-light.

We could?

Ivy would have said yes. She had never danced with her father. But Joseph was reaching for her: he was saying her name. Ivy stood with an apologetic smile, the colours of Angus and Marina glinting past as she began to dance, letting music flow along her bloodstream: an easeful piano, a low clarinet. She moved, lifting her arms above her head: these were not the gestures they had been taught in school, those timid positions of toe and elbow. This was free dancing, Joseph and Frances and her dancing apart, alone and together, Ivy lost in the day as it became evening, a freshness coming to her from the open windows, the grass gathering moisture. Joseph took her arms for a moment and they danced together, Ivy proud to have such a radiant brother, his face alive with happiness.

She had always enjoyed dancing, and now – in a single swoop of feeling – she wondered if it could be her mode of life, if she could dance herself around the world, under spotlights. What a way to live: to dance through it, such focus in the body, and to be watched: she saw that Bear was sitting now, at a distance from Gilbert on the sofa, his gaze on her.

Ivy felt much as she had, only a few years ago, turning cartwheels over the lawn, her family blurring, that quick necessity of her bones; were they not created for this? But here was the edge of the sofa and here the softness of the rug under her bare feet. Here: a stumble, of a sort, and she was on Bear's lap, his hands on her, catching her, it could be said. This was the most she had been touched all day; the most she had ever been touched, perhaps, by another person. And so: she existed, after all. She was here. And not only this: the whole room was in Bear's hands, in their touch as they moved now, just slightly, as though to hold her in place. Everyone was looking, she knew, at this and only this. For now, and now – one second, two – Easter Day was hers.

The music stopped. It was Marina by the gramophone, her eyes dark and wet. Then her voice, distant and high, as though it came from outside her.

That's enough now, don't you think? We must think of supper. And we haven't shown our guest her room!

A beat of silence: the group moved towards the change. Ivy stood up, Bear's hands, loose, falling from her like water.

Yes! Ivy felt snapped to attention, a flush building across her entire body.

Marina smiled, her lips a tight band around her face. She lowered her voice.

Where is Anne?

Marina turned to leave, gesturing for Ivy to follow. Frances nodded at Joseph, as though to a partner at a formal dance. Gilbert and Bear, in their places at the ends of the sofa, stared at the floor. Angus was nowhere to be seen.

Take Frances to her room, please, Ivy? Her suitcase is in the hallway.

The house became unknown to Ivy in this young woman's presence, containing new shadows, unexpected turns as she led her up the stairs. Frances had been given the front guest room, the best they had. Two windows to the garden, solid furniture, an air of patient waiting, as though it had missed everything that happened downstairs, had only traces of lamb scent, a sense of an evening passed, lost for ever. There was something embarrassing about standing in this room with Frances, the space somehow too small for two, though it was a large, wide room, the bed in a floral quilt between them.

Ivy saw a flash of limbs and clothing: Joseph and Frances in another bed, as perhaps they had been, their arms around each other, the world turning over with their touch. Ivy made herself stiff, polite, pointing out the bureau and jug on the night stand, describing the way to the water closet at the end of the hallway. But Frances seemed perfectly at ease, placing her red suitcase on the chest of drawers, looking at each painting on the wall with care.

And where's your room?

Oh, it's just – we'll pass it – I can show you, if you like—

As soon as Ivy said this she remembered that it was not tidy, that there might be undergarments in a pile on the floor, that her bed could be in disarray. Perhaps Anne— but she had been so busy, cooking and cleaning, not dancing with them of course but boiling water, washing plates and cups in the sink. For every step down the creaking corridor Ivy crossed her fingers, and when the door opened to smooth bedcovers she felt gratitude bloom across her. She would kiss Anne later, she vowed. She would rub her shoulders.

These are beautiful, Ivy.

Frances was peering at some paintings Ivy had done a year ago, perhaps more, on thick card tacked to the walls: flowers folded in on themselves, something melancholy, almost deathly, in the hang of their necks.

Oh, those are nothing—

Ivy knew her paintings were skilled enough, but they would never hang in museums, as Marina's and Angus's would. They would not be looked at again in even five years, except by Anne when she came to clean.

No, they're really good—

Ivy felt uncomfortable, as though partly undressed. She had begun to understand what made her paintings so fleeting, destined for the tide of detritus that swept the world. They were nothing new, and newness is what made creativity, she thought, or perhaps in some cases it could be a heightening of what already existed, a stretching of it—

Frances was looking at her. The two of them smiled at each other, for a moment, the sky lilac at the open window, the call of a bird sounding from deep in the garden. The room stood around them: it widened as it watched them.

Anne was making cocoa, the milk's steam marking the final end of brandy, and music: the day would end roundly, after all, two siblings and their mother by the fire, only Frances to make the night differ from any other Easter Sunday. Would Ivy not wake up tomorrow, and face a day like any other? She had a whole life to figure out, and nothing but the expanse of days; there were decisions to be made, Marina never ceased to remind her. What would she be? Or would she only be herself, as she was now: daughter of Marina and

Gilbert, sister of Joseph? She could live only in relation to others, in the stillness of the garden, in the heavy breath of her bedroom. One by one, her days would pass, and she would live in them. Perhaps this was enough?

Gilbert and Bear had left hours before: Gilbert brisk, seemingly pleased to be getting into his car and motoring away. He had slung his work bag on his shoulder and kissed Ivy once on each cheek. Next to Gilbert, Bear was notice-ably languid, his every gesture prolonged: his kiss to Ivy was singular, almost nonchalant. They had waved the car away, and for a second Ivy had thought of being a stowaway, of how it would feel to be lying against the deep smell of Gilbert's leather seats, feeling the countryside disappear behind her.

Afterwards, they sat at the kitchen table: Joseph and Frances with their chairs pulled close to one another, Ivy opposite them, Marina facing the stove as Anne poured powder into milk, stirred the mixture with a wooden spoon. Marina did not mind watching Anne at work, but it had always given Ivy a sense of abstract irritation, made her unable to stay still. As a child she would insist on *helping*, standing on a chair with a wooden spoon while Anne invented things for her to do, tip-ping a little sauce into a pan that was not on the heat, chopping soft fruit with a blunt knife.

Joseph was telling stories from university: he was bright-eyed with brandy, restless, his leg jogging under the table.

And that was when Mivs brought a cow's head into the JCR! Dripping with blood, all over the floor—

As she sipped the cocoa, Ivy began to feel sleep creeping at the edges of her thoughts, but she did not panic. She would sleep, and she would wake again. *And Frances would still be here.* A whole day could not hold everything, after all. One needed to fall into rest, and rise again, to understand anything.

How about it, Ivy?

Joseph was looking at her; they all were. Joseph had a new intensity in his expression, a look that reminded her of days when he would dare her to climb to the roof, or run barefoot through a patch of thistles. Marina's face, in contrast, had dulled, her own fatigue, perhaps, her dread at another portion of the evening unforeseen. And Frances was smiling, always smiling, looking at Joseph with such clear happiness, her mouth very slightly open, her hands curled around her cup of cocoa. At university, Joseph had written to Marina, he and Frances campaigned together – for the republicans in the Spanish Civil War, against all forms of fascism – and Ivy could imagine Frances following him to any cause he believed in. Whatever it was that Joseph was proposing, Ivy wanted to say yes, if only for her.

A swim then? The three of us? I know Mater won't manage it, not at this time of year—

Marina pulled herself to her full height, but said nothing. It was a tradition, of sorts, for Ivy and Joseph to go for the first swim of the year together, usually much later: in June or even July.

But – won't the water be too cold?

Ivy was trying to imagine it: wearing a bathing costume, when she had already pulled a jersey over her linen dress.

People swim in the Isis when it's frozen!

Joseph lifted his arm from around Frances's shoulders, his gestures rushed, powered by impatience. There was no question of refusal, when Joseph was like this, his energy surging around the room, like a bee looking for escape. Marina shifted in her chair.

You go with Ivy, Joseph – let Frances keep me company here?

Disappointment passed through Joseph's features, but Marina was already reaching – a slight stretch – her slender fingers patting Frances's arm.

We haven't had much of a chance to talk, have we, dear?

But Frances hasn't even seen the river, Mother—

Marina did not counter this; it would have been rude, somehow. And so the decision seemed to fall, as the whole day had, on Frances. Ivy and Joseph watched her: Ivy knew their eagerness was similar – people were always remarking on the matching set of their mouths, the persuasive intensity of their shared eyebrows. And there was a moment – Ivy felt it, like a breeze passing through the room – when Frances considered coming with them. For years Ivy would think of what it would have been like, had she been there. She could feel the textures of that alternative night almost as clearly as the one that rolled out, that rolled away from her, faster and faster, as though there was no other choice to be made.

I'll stay with Marina, you two go—

Perhaps Frances did not like swimming in cold water, did not want to venture out into a strange wood, when she had already come to a house where she knew only Joseph, endured overcooked food, stranger after stranger staring at her, appraising her. Joseph shook his head a little, as though to adjust.

Righto, you ready then, Ive?

He could not refuse his own request any more than she could. They would swim; it was Easter Sunday. They had not gone to church but would do this: lower themselves into water, immerse themselves in it, their own kind of baptism.

Ivy had pulled on a bathing costume under her dress, and dragged the jersey back over it. She had tied up her hair. As soon as they were outside she felt it all rushing towards her: the garden, the woods and the river beyond it. Everything smelt so much, after the house: there were millions of insects out here, and plants, an entire universe, while the inside was so simple. Why had they spent most of the day in there, surrounded only by themselves? Sometimes she imagined she would live in that house for ever, and wondered if it would be so terrible. *A beautiful house*, people were always saying. *Paradise.* But it was the garden that was her home, more than the house was, covered with her mother's fabrics and artworks, every room thick with the breath of her, of Angus. She passed a tree where she and Joseph used to sit as children, two branches forming a double seat – our *throne*, they would say. When other children came they made them pages and ladies-in-waiting, sent them to fetch bouquets of daisies, single blackberries balanced on leaf plates. Ivy had the sense, back then, that the garden was *with* them: that she, Joseph and the trees and grasses were all of a kind.

When she glanced back Ivy saw the studio lit with a few shaded lamps, a deep red glow with Angus at its centre. Joseph was ahead of her, already, his leaping steps like hers in a dream where she moved too fast, was thrown from one new landscape to another. She ran a little, to catch him up. The smooth lawns of the garden gave way to the waving grasses of the meadow, then they too seemed to shoot past, to deepen into the green-brown of the woods, these familiar trees always unknown again in darkness. In the wood there was a slow inhalation, the sense of being watched, a need to move more carefully amongst the undergrowth, the fallen bodies of long-dead trees. Smooth garlands of leaves ran against Ivy's arm, already slick with evening.

What a night!

Joseph had stopped, was looking through the trees to where the sky was spread and clear, its wash of stars the surprise they always were. They used to have a telescope, but Ivy never felt there was a better view than this: the naked eye presented with this distant, unfurling garden, the moon like a shy bystander.

Can you smell it? The river?

Joseph had his nose lifted, like a hound; he seemed so brotherly in that moment that Ivy wanted to hug him, to wrap her arms around his body as though it were one of the trees that surrounded them: she felt certain he would feel as solid, that at his core a thick trunk grew instead of a spine. No wonder Frances loved him. And she realized she could already smell the river: its green, tangled rush, its complicated call to the future.

Come on, Ive—

He reached out his hand now. She took it, and they walked through the rest of the woods in this way, leaning partly on each other.

At the river, Ivy undressed slowly, placing her clothes in a pile on a tree stump. She could not see the water, but could hear its voice, the low sound of a long journey. Beside her, Joseph was already naked – he only ever swam naked – the familiar soft contours of his chest giving way to a place she looked away from. He turned, and she saw only the boyish, comical division of his buttocks.

There was a place where the bank sloped, just slightly, to allow them to step down instead of jump. In the height of summer, in the brightness of daytime, they did jump, with glee, with shrieking. But this swim was something more serious: even Joseph moved slowly, gasping as his feet entered the water.

Is it cold?

Ivy shouted this, pointlessly, but Joseph did not answer.

His legs were in now, his breathing hard and fast. Ivy was only a few feet behind: as her toes touched the water she felt like an Arctic explorer in one of Gilbert's travel books. What was this, if not ice? The cold spread to her knees now, as she waded; it claimed her thighs, her pelvis, her stomach. She was giving herself to a devil, she felt; hell was surely not heat after all but cold, this alien element, so harsh to flesh. Ahead of her, Joseph was swimming, his head steady above the water, his arms rising like great fish with every stroke.

It's not as bad when you swim—

She lowered her whole body, the cold becoming abstract, so intense it was total, encompassing everything. She was nothing but cold now, and so could bear it, this new cold self, cold the only element she had ever known, would ever know.

I'm getting used to it!

She called to Joseph, as though they were only in a cool summer swimming pool, hoping he would come closer. He was only a few feet away, but they were in the mangled part of the river now; she could feel reeds soft as snakes wrapping against her legs, the base of the river becoming jumbled, neither solid ground nor pure water, a mass of growth and decay. She swam through the soft binds as they had learnt to, neither struggling nor giving in, continuing, facing straight. She had almost reached him.

Ahead of them the sky was changing. Ivy's first thought was dawn, though this made no sense. But there was a light, unquestionably increasing in brightness, moving towards them, steady with intention.

Joseph?

She felt him stop, begin to tread water.

For her whole life, she would wonder how to describe the light. It was not like a torch beam or a lantern. It had neither the gentleness of fire nor the simple glow of electricity. It was a sound, as well as a light, and more than this: it was feeling, pressing and shifting, a pattern that moved and seemed to move her with it. She could hear Joseph close beside her now, his nervous laughter, his swearing, but it was as though he was on another planet, where people spoke and had voices, and she was in a different, silent place, of light and sensation. The world of objects – of chairs and dresses, of teacups and paintings and flowers – was only a facade, she knew in that moment. There was another world, a place she had never even considered.

Ivy would not be able to say, even to herself, what made this light so different from all those she had ever seen before. It was an animal, she would have said, if she knew of any animal that moved or looked anything like it. It was a creature from elsewhere, she felt, without asking herself what that meant. It was visiting.

Or— She looked again, one long, last, greedy look, in which she felt that the light was a person, in some way, was love itself—

Ivy—

Joseph was calling, his voice constricted, high-pitched. He was behind her now; calling her back. But the light was doing something new, moving in a rhythm she could only describe as *dancing*. She watched it, surely only for a few seconds, willing herself into that pure, formless place. She turned to Joseph: had he felt it too? But she saw only the river, flat and imperious. A still black pool.

Joseph?

She took a deep breath. The light had gone, even the stars seemed dimmer. Joseph was playing a game, she knew: he had done that before, hovering just below the surface to emerge again, like a whale in a sparkling spray, blowing water from his mouth. She went under.

Here was the time of nothing: here were the drift of reeds, the acres of cold darkness with no human voice. Here was the long existence of their childhood, one paused day they would always inhabit, the layers of water and earth and sediment becoming time itself, every day they had come here, every day they could come again. Ivy was a fish, now: pushing deeper, about to find Joseph, turning in her own element, her body smooth and searching. But there was no long-bodied brother here, no joke waiting to be revealed.

He would be on the bank, she realized: laughing, his hair dripping, one of Anne's rough-washed towels wrapped around him. Of course he would. She surfaced, gasping, water pouring from her. She was freezing, she realized. She might never be warm again. She looked to the bank, to where she knew she would see Joseph waiting for her, as he had waited all his life: pausing on his own bicycle, aged seven, as she pushed hers up the dusty hill behind him. Standing at the edge of the river, at the edge of the woods, over and over, reaching out his hand. She could see him, at all his ages, and – almost – as he was, a grown man, stunned as he must be, panting with cold, his hair bedraggled.

But there was no Joseph. There was only the world: bank and tree and round, dull moon, looking straight through her, indifferent.

DAY TWO

April 1938

She had missed the first five minutes of the funeral, the drone of a hymn as she approached the church, the flattened opening words. She had not planned to come at all, but sitting at the back she was not there, exactly: she was watching. She could see every person, every back, but no one – except Reverend Giles, perhaps – could see her. She was used to ignoring him, to watching the church instead: the windows with their underwater colours, the ceiling covered in engraved stars. When she was younger, Gilbert had taken her to church most Sundays, and still insisted on it occasionally, despite his agnosticism. *It is proper*, he had said simply. She remembered the yawning boredom of those mornings: empty time, as she thought of it, the space above the pulpit where dust moved in clouds, the boom of the organ.

She tried to look up, around, anywhere but ahead. Reverend Giles was standing next to her brother's empty coffin, and talking in the same voice he used to announce the winner of the largest marrow at the harvest festival. His voice was like too-bright sunshine: Ivy winced.

A respectable and learned young man. A tribute to his loving parents.

Bear was sitting with Angus at the front. Ivy watched their

necks as though there was something to be learned from them, their thickness next to Marina's, the thin pole of her, held completely straight. Ivy thought she saw her mother's shoulders shudder, just once, such a quick movement that she doubted whether it had happened at all. Afterwards, Marina was entirely still again, pale and upright, a line of light. She did not move as Ivy's father scrambled to his feet from the adjacent pew, taking a notecard from his pocket.

Gilbert seemed to have prepared a speech fit for a wedding: he spoke of Joseph as if he still existed, was about to sit up from the coffin, after all, and laugh at them.

A huge boy, Gilbert said. *First of all we must say this.*

He lifted his hand to his mouth, as though exclaiming again at the size of his son. He touched his lower lip, frowned and continued.

The doctors said they had hardly seen a baby so large. Screaming and red, head full of hair.

He touched his own hair, now, as though for illustration. Again, Ivy thought she saw her mother move and return to stillness, off-on, like a familiar semaphore only she could see.

. . . And from the beginning: fond of japes. A rascal. But a thoughtful son, always writing letters back from university. Kind to his sister. Nearly always.

Gilbert stopped here. He cast the briefest of glances at the coffin. He looked at Marina, who did not move. He seemed to squint towards the back, towards Ivy. He was so short-sighted, she doubted he could see her. *Kind to his sister.* Ivy wanted, all of a sudden, for Reverend Giles to speak again, for the bleaching blandness of his voice to cover them all. *Stand up, silly man*, she urged him silently. *Rescue Father.*

But it was Angus who stood, gliding past Marina in his black suit, the straight line of his shoulders pointing towards the coffin. He put a hand on Gilbert's back. *Come on. Good man, good man.* Gilbert was bending: he was small, beneath Angus, as though suddenly elderly, being moved to his seat. Ivy found that she could barely see – she was crying, perhaps, or had simply gone blind. Or: she was unable to watch. She had heard this phrase before without knowing what it meant. She had always wanted to see everything.

The whole place seemed to moisten, to curve inward. Ivy was not crying, she assured herself. It was everyone else who moved hands to their eyes, their mouths, reached for handkerchiefs. Several of the men coughed briskly. And here at last was Reverend Giles, urging them to stand up, to sing. Ivy doubted whether she could move her legs, if standing was still something that could be done, by a girl such as her. But then she was upright, after all, holding a hymn book in her hands.

Outside, the grass was so bright it seemed impossible that death existed, that anyone could die. Here instead were groups of people in their smart clothes, moving through the world as they always did, towards food and drink, to their next need or relief. Ivy stood in the breeze, having no idea where to go, the air of the world seeming to hold her too briefly before passing her by. It was Bear, in his greatcoat – surely too warm for this weather, the thick sleeve touching her mac – who steered her. She felt his weight at her side, slow and heavy, a ship, became aware of Angus there too, the three of them moving over the electric-green lawn towards—

A grave. A space in the earth.

Bear ducked his head to hers: she smelt his aftershave, and something lower, of night-time: whisky. He seemed to be asking if she still wanted to go, if she was sure. She couldn't remember having been asked at all, and yet now she nodded. She was curious, she found, about the void, the emptiness, though when they arrived it looked almost ordinary, some-how horticultural, the lips of the turf rolled away to reveal only more soil, threaded with roots. Her mother was not here, she saw blankly, or her father either. Bear and Angus and Ivy: like strange comrades of some kind, reaching into a jug which held flowers, for a reason that Ivy could not understand. Then Bear again: the warmth of his breath, the peaty lace of booze.

They're for the— Coffin. We put them—

His voice died away. The flowers were daffodils, Ivy regis-tered now. And of course she thought of Easter, of another girl who looked like her, crouching down in a wood filled with birdsong. But then she remembered the prize. Joseph must have been ten or eleven: Marina had taken her to see him reciting the whole of Wordsworth's poem at school, his voice wavering but clear, like a glass of water, the room bright around him. She thought of the straightness of his back, when he was called on stage again to receive the small, golden trophy. *Best Poetry Recital, 1928.*

And here was the coffin, manoeuvred on ropes, pulled on strings like a puppet. It hovered above the hole for a moment, as though deciding whether to go further. She had heard Marina, yesterday, asking what would make it heavy, if there was no body, her tone wilder and wilder until Angus was forced to answer: *Bricks*, his voice a strange bark, not his own. Ivy had expected a scream to follow this, her ear pressed against the rough wood of the kitchen door, but there was only silence. To the bricks – ordinary house bricks, Ivy had been appalled to see this morning – they had added some *mementoes*, as the undertaker had called them, his mouth pursed around the word. A photograph of Joseph in the garden as a young child, taken by Marina, a china statue of a dog – his favourite thing at the time – held to his cheek. One of the political pamphlets he and Frances had produced at Oxford. A small teddy bear he had barely treasured; Marina had insisted on keeping Joseph's beloved, one-eared Ted, whom Joseph had still slept with occasionally, when he was unwell, or homesick.

The coffin swayed – too light after all, perhaps – looking as though it might miss the grave, sail instead over the grass, onwards into its own obscure eternity. But it made the grave, at last, was lowered, nestled there. The world slanted, tipped: Ivy put her hand to her mouth. She would not vomit. She would have liked to have fainted, to simply disappear. Perhaps she would fall into the grave itself, a dramatic gesture she felt certain she had seen before, in a film perhaps. But instead she found herself flinging the flowers, throwing them away from herself, towards the symbol of her brother. She did not want to see them land, she found. But there they were: their yellow like a voice, something speaking for Joseph, instead of him, when he would never speak again.

At Cressingdon, Anne had been cooking since dawn: there were sea creatures – mussels, tiny prawns – suspended in jellies (Joseph would have hated them) and a bird pie. In the garden room the food was already ransacked, abandoned, a few slices left of the pie, a single mollusc still floating in its artificial sea. *People are always hungry at funerals*, Anne had said earlier; Marina looked sharply at her but said nothing. She had barely eaten since Easter.

Life was emptied, Ivy knew now: it was objects again. Tables and chairs and people, her body taking its place in the air, speaking, turning. People saying things to her – commiserations, their hands on her arm – and her replies. This would continue, she supposed, for ever, until the same darkness that covered Joseph's head – in some unknown place – covered her own, and the objects and people and talking passed over her. She wondered if the unknown made her grief particular; if she had been able to hold one of his drowned hands, would this soothe her pain, or only intensify it? Perhaps it was better, not to have to imagine him rotting in the ground, his face slowly turning into earth. She only knew that loss, for her, had become merged with mystery: there was that desperate feeling when you lose something in the house, feel yourself tormented by the simple frustration, life held still until its finding.

Now, she stood in a corner, hoping to blend with the walls. Marina had made her wear her dark grey dress, although she had wanted the blue, Joseph's favourite, and surely a sad enough colour. She considered putting the last sea creature in her mouth, just for the disgust of it, to feel it, dead and pickled on her tongue. She would drink, perhaps, as Bear had been doing, and laugh loudly, feel the whole room turn to stare at her.

Ivy swerved around a large, scented aunt – *a tragedy, my poor girl* – and then a huddled group who spoke before they saw her – she only heard *no body found* – *days* – *the river* – before she walked, holding herself rigid, into the drawing room, looking for brandy on the high shelves, only moving her eyes. But here was Marina, sitting on the rose settee, and next to her: Frances. Frances herself, present as any other person, her legs crossed, her hands in her lap. Then she was standing up, Joseph's girl, present and breathing. She was opening her arms. She held Ivy for a second: she smelt of cold cream, and bird pie. When Ivy did not move, or speak,

Frances let go; she wavered for a moment, before sitting back down, her eyes pooling with tears.

On Marina's other side, Angus was static, stiff, his head handsome as a portrait. Every few seconds, Marina patted his hand, as though reassuring herself he was still there. Ivy looked back to Frances. She was unmistakably the girl who had eaten while they all watched, who had danced with Joseph just feet away from the place where they all now sat. She was the same girl who had looked at Ivy's paintings, who had turned away with light in her eyes. And yet it did not seem that she could be Frances, any more: that light was gone. Her hair was brushed but flat, her eyes ringed with blue-white shadows.

She is so free, Joseph had told Ivy, the day he died. *She is so alive.* He had described a coat she had, navy blue with gold buttons. Every one of the buttons, he said, was engraved with a different animal. The top one, he said – his voice softening, he was almost blushing – was a lion.

Here was the girl, and here was the coat, just as he had described. It must have been the smartest thing she owned, her mother's even, preserved in mothballs in a vicarage wardrobe. Ivy could see the animals, as vital as her brother had said. They seemed to be almost dancing, twirling in a line down the fabric. But Frances was neither free, nor alive. Ivy found herself feeling angered by this: how dare she appear to die, when her brother was truly dead, and nothing could save him. She remembered Frances the night she came back from the river, alone: she had been a dream figure, a form barely contained, a rush of colour and movement. Frances had held Marina; Ivy remembered that, the shape of them, one being in the darkness. Ivy had stood beside them, shivering in a blanket, unable to get warm.

Angus had something in his hands. A service sheet, Ivy could see now, a sketched likeness as its back cover. She had been too late at the service, to see this, the image of Joseph as clear as any other. Angus had done the sketch on a summer morning before Joseph went to university. She remembered them in the studio, Joseph shirtless and laughing, the light orange, jocular, Angus with the wireless on, more relaxed than usual, a board on his knees. He had captured Joseph's eyes exactly: the way they both creased and shined when he was happy, creating a general benevolence, a look of love that could feel personal to whoever saw it.

Dear Joseph, Marina said now, touching the image, her voice toneless, walking along a fine wire.

He was so kind.

The shell of Frances's features fell open, her mouth softening, collapsing. She held a handkerchief there as though to close it, let out a brief hiccup of a sob. Marina pursed her lips.

Ivy felt the rounding, repellent push of her mother's presence. She had noticed how closely it matched the opposite feeling she had throughout her childhood, of wanting to be next to her, constantly. She remembered mornings walking through the house attached to her mother's waist, her arms like a vice, refusing to let go. The smell of her skin, her clothes. The number of times she allowed herself to be painted, just to feel it: her mother's attention moving over her, the warmth of it, like a volcano. Ivy shifted, spoke without planning to—

I've just got to – check on something. Anne asked me—

Her mother nodded. She was only too happy, Ivy knew, for Anne to be helped. Only one servant, for everything! It was not what Marina had grown up to expect. It made her uneasy, even if this itself created its own discomfort. Every few months, before Joseph died, Marina would rage through the house, screaming at Angus, at Ivy, at Anne. Nobody could do enough. How could she paint, in this pigsty? It was inconceivable.

She *would* help Anne, Ivy thought now – it was the only thing she could imagine, plunging her hands in hot water and cold, being softened by the steam of the kitchen. She moved towards the clatter of dishes, the smell of soap.

But somebody had her hand. She was being pulled, like a child, into the hallway, the empty cool hallway with its segments of light. Beyond the wall, there was noise, the weight of bodies and conversation. But here, there was only air, a wooden floor and: Bear, wearing a suit, his hair in his eyes.

What are you doing?

He held a finger to his lips. He still had her hand, and he lifted it to his mouth now: he kissed it, his lips tickling her knuckles. His eyes, she saw, were full of water, brimming like goldfish bowls. Tears, she had decided, were stupid: they achieved nothing. Hadn't she cried, on that first night, and what had it done?

I have to— She tried to pull away, but he kept her there, staring, one hand on her waist now.

Please, Ivy.

She felt something tug within her: a subterranean movement, a pulse that she recognized from Easter Day, something living within her, still. Bear's breath was beside her ear now, damp, quickening.

I need you.

And he had his hands on her, at her waist, on her back, was moving them in a way that felt like her life emptying, and filling again, like having Joseph here, and then losing him. No one entered the hallway: only the trees watched from the one tall window, waving and bowing as though it were nothing. He kissed her, his lips practised, gliding, intercepting hers at precise points, lifting, parting, pressing. Ivy thought of the boys at school dances, who held her forearms and pointed their tongues. Kissing them was like stumbling into a wet, dark cave, but this was closer to music, to dancing. And there was something about Bear's mouth, the taste of him: sweet and layered, new and old all at once. Rather than wondering why he was kissing her, she now wondered why Bear had never kissed her before. Why they had not been kissing for years. There was something in this pleasure that seemed greater than other sensations, significant in some way, as though she was being handed something weighty and valuable, a solid paperweight placed in her palm.

Bear pulled away.

Thank you, he said.

No, thank you, she almost replied, but it was too funny, the thought of laughter abstract, as food was when she was not hungry. She remembered laughing at an old uncle's funeral when she was a child, Angus carrying her out through the back. And with this memory came her answer: of course they had never kissed before. It was laughable, in fact, that they should kiss. He was a *dear friend* of her parents, and even more than this, it was rumoured, to Angus. Joseph had told her this once, when he'd had sherry after dinner, speaking at the side of his mouth. *Proper sweethearts*, he'd said. *In the war.* One of Angus's many lovers, now absorbed into the family, tolerated, at least, by Marina. She had even found them both farm work, so they could avoid conscription. Ivy struggled to imagine it: Angus, a young man, digging in the dirt.

She remembered Joseph's face, at Easter. *Bit old for you.* But Joseph was gone: they had stood together, little more than an hour ago, and thrown flowers on his empty coffin. They had dropped them down, as though they were children, playing a game.

Bear was standing away from her, now: he was looking. Ivy hated her mother, then, for making her wear the grey sack which swallowed her waist, made her legs look like two pegs. She wished she was wearing something tight, something that held her at the waist, as he did. She wanted to reach for him again; she amazed herself, with her wanting of this. She put her hand out, unable to say it, to ask.

Through the wall, she heard her name mentioned, quietly, more loudly, and then Anne was in the hall with them, and it was an entirely different place.

Your mother's looking for you.

Anne said this to Ivy but looked at Bear, frowning. *Come along,* she said then, her voice dense with suppressed feeling – for the second time that day Ivy found herself taken by the arm, and pulled away.

Ivy was washing dishes, after all, the suds soft on her hands, the soap fragrant, every sensation simply a memory of kissing, every pleasantry mirrored by the thought of Bear's smell, his taste, the skin of his neck just above his collar. She shivered. It was like lowering her head beneath bathwater, beauty just below the surface of every moment. She remembered Bear's look before he kissed her: frank, practised, the moment loosened already, eternal, its seconds pictures she could turn over in her mind. She felt a pull, as clear as the tide beneath her as she sat at the edge of the sea when she was five, trailing her fingers in damp sand. She would find him again, and they would kiss. She knew kissing Bear would not change the day, but it could quieten things, perhaps, muffle the shouting voice that had lived within her since Easter, still barely two weeks ago, that had made her, at certain moments, want to leave her own body, as Joseph had, to simply float away.

From the garden, she thought she heard Bear's voice, then the brief, dog-like greeting of his laugh. Anne glanced up too; Ivy knew she could not leave immediately, could not be drawn to the sound like a whistle. She forced herself to finish cleaning the last of the glasses, doing it sloppily, suds still visible at their bases.

I had better see where Father is, she said, feeling that enough time had passed. Anne looked up.

Just — be careful, Ivy, love. A pause, Anne wringing a wet cloth in her hands.

You're in a funny place. It's — a funeral.

Of course.

Ivy nodded as she left the room, seeing Anne's face lower back to the sink. But it was no kind of funeral, Ivy had decided, without a body to bury, for someone who shouldn't even be dead, who might not even— But she had promised herself not to think that, not again.

She could not go to the garden, not now, when it was so busy with people, so bright with daytime. Instead, she went towards the studio: Bear had been known to sleep there, in the middle of parties, pillow-less and splayed on the chaise longue, his head tipped back, one hand dropping off its edge.

She admired this ability, to simply be able to close his eyes, and drop into oblivion, anywhere he pleased.

The studio felt forbidden, hushed, the blinds down, only a brief shape of brightness visible at their edges. This was where Marina and Angus spent most of their time, where time itself seemed to halt for them. How to describe the way they worked together? Like cats, Ivy had thought: their ease, their prowling. The wordless acceptance of routine: you stand here, I will sit there.

The fire was unlit: the room was cool. The Buddha sat on the mantelpiece, immovable in his private contemplation, the smallest of smiles on his lips. He was apart from the clutter that surrounded him, the postcards and family photographs that appeared incidental but had been there for years. There were squat ceramic jars, painted by Marina, a black-and-white photograph of her as a young girl. And above all this: two paintings by Angus, vases floating in a constant summer field.

Ivy moved towards the chaise longue, remembering without wanting to all the close, adhesive hours of childhood she had spent in here, being painted, watching painting, and eventually: painting herself. There was one of her recent works pinned to the outside of the mantelpiece, as though an afterthought. A clutch of pansies, their folds labial, neither quite lifelike nor depicting something beyond life, as Marina and Angus's paintings did. Ivy recognized her own failure and was unmoved by it; she was used to the sensation by now, its texture smoothed by familiarity: it glided by.

There was material, bunched in the gloom: as Ivy went closer it moved, took shape. Her heart did its soaring, separate from her, its own master. But it was Gilbert, not Bear: his hair disturbed, his tie loosened, dress trousers straining over his middle. Ivy tried not to feel disappointed. It was her father, after all, who she had comforted in those bare days following Joseph's disappearance, before they had given up hope. She had lain a flannel on his head, held his hand. Ivy had felt the way that caring could separate her mind, for a few minutes, leaving her body light, free from all the thinking that dragged it down. She had seen the way that days could become blue tunnels, spaces that barely had air enough to breathe.

Ivy? Is that you?

She thought Gilbert had been sleeping, but as she went closer she saw the disorder of his features, his eyes seeming to meet his mouth in wetness: he had been crying.

Daddy?

Ivy, dear, do come here.

He reached out a hand, and she held it, lowered herself down next to him. For minutes, neither of them spoke. Even in the midst of her caring, Ivy had sensed herself at a distance from her father. She sometimes felt that they were standing on either side of a deep stream, calling out, unable to hear. It was Joseph who was closest to him, Joseph who Gilbert sent books to, long letters meant to inform his education. She suspected that her father thought her unintellectual, like

Angus and Marina, but without their talent to compensate.

How are you bearing up, Rabs? Rabs had been his pet name for her since early childhood, when she spent long dry days catching wild rabbits, attempting to tame them. That was back when Gilbert lived with them, when the afternoon room at Cressingdon was his study, filled with the smells of pipe smoke, sweat and tea. She remembered running to him with a particularly deep rabbit-scratch, the way he distract-edly applied a bandage, returned to his books without speaking. The house must have been almost empty, she thinks now, for her to choose him.

I'm managing, thank you, Daddy. Managing was the word she had chosen, for answering questions like these. It implied distress, but also resilience. It ended conversations, she had found: it stopped them cold. But her father carried on.

I know how close you – you must be – but I never – I never want you to blame yourself.

This phrase had been repeated several times since Joseph's death: by Angus, Genevieve, Hector, by everyone but her mother. Marina had not blamed Ivy, exactly, but did not seem to mind if she blamed herself. In the days of the search – torches flashing at the windows of Cressingdon through the night – the police had asked her the same questions, over and over: had she seen Joseph drowning? Could he have climbed out, somehow? But Ivy could not say anything that helped. She had only told them about the light days later, and most of them seemed to pay little attention. A light was irrelevant to a drowning, it seemed, of a different element, though Ivy wondered if it would have seemed more important coming from anyone but her, a still-shivering young girl, her eyes blackened by lack of sleep. Even Gilbert, after an initial flicker of interest, seemed to disregard it. It was not the sky that had killed Joseph, after all, but the earth: water and mud and vines, a swamping denseness so opaque it must have swallowed him for ever. But it was light Ivy saw in her dreams, its beam on and off the cold, calm river, with no part of Joseph emerging, no glimpse of the skin of a forearm, an elbow. She had woken, for weeks, believing the river was all around her, filling her room, leaving her unable to breathe. And then, often, some sense of the light would come to her: soothing, almost, abstract, as if all of life was in those first moments of wakening.

Now, Ivy stared at the blinds, wondering when they could be lifted. Before, this room was always flooded with light: Angus got those glass doors put in, and the sun filled the room like a pool, it was *like swimming in light*, Marina used to say. *Like heaven itself*, she said, though Ivy knew she didn't believe in heaven. She touched her father's hand, an attempt at reassurance, felt the thinness of his skin, the way it only seemed to coat the bone, as a shawl covers a chair. It was separate to his body, it seemed, not all of a piece with it, like her own.

I don't blame myself, Daddy. Don't worry. It was so easy to lie, she had found, once you began.

Good girl, Gilbert said. He closed his eyes, and tears fell down his cheeks. He didn't move: he didn't wipe them away. There was a noise: a faint shuffle, a door swinging open.

Hullo?

It was Angus, marching to the blinds, pulling them up with one motion. Ivy felt scalded: she lifted her hands to her eyes.

Good God, Angus, steady on. Gilbert was rubbing his face with his sleeve now, he was standing up, straightening himself. The room was transformed: it seemed clinically bright, the sun an interrogation. Angus was like a visitor from a country where people wore smooth, unrumpled clothes, where they combed their hair.

What are you doing? Angus's voice sounded hedged, protective; in the corner, under a pale sheet, was a huge canvas of his, left for weeks. It would be his masterwork, Marina had said. It would make *his star shine even brighter.* Ivy had only seen glimpses: the figure of a man, silver-blue, something Greek about his majesty. She remembered the heaviness of Angus's head above her as he showed her how to hold a brush: she must have been four or five. But he had never fooled her that she had any talent for it. *Try dancing*, he'd said, when she was twelve, and she did. She had tried to dance, then act, and sing, and write. She was a *dilettante*: she knew it as soon as she heard the word, at one of her mother's dinner parties. She held the knowledge inside her, kept it still, unmoving.

There's tea now – in the garden. Angus gestured out, to the shining day, the garden beyond, guests beginning to move

67

across the bright stage of the grass, dark paper outlines, blown by the breeze. Gilbert nodded.

Jolly good.

But nobody began to leave. The three of them were still, in their peculiar triad: father, daughter, some version of a stepfather, the three of them separate and quiet together. Through the windows, the sun was warm, softened by the fabric that surrounded them, the paintings on the walls seeming to answer the light. Ivy remembered icons she had seen in candlelit, incense-wreathed churches in Italy as a child: figures of the Trinity, how gentle they seemed, their long bodies, their haloes of gold.

She thought of Bear, then – another long body – of the hair on the backs of his hands, those same hands reaching for his neck, his casual apprehension of his own form. The warmth of his waist, the sweetness of his mouth: was this not light too, of a kind? She was ashamed of her wanting, and yet here it was – the stepping of it deep within her, like fingers on a piano, paying no mind to her shame.

There was a danger, as they emerged, in the settling gauze of the afternoon across the garden, a fear Ivy felt almost as moisture, seeping from the ground. Small groups sat on the lawn, one person lying, a hand across their eyes, another half-reclined beside a teacup, a cherry tart. The danger seemed to come from absence: the fact that Joseph was in none of these groups, that he never would be. *Never would be.* Ivy glanced at Gilbert, in case he would collapse, somehow, from her own thoughts. But he was moving, with apparent ease, towards the tea table. He was lifting a cup, without thinking, perhaps, that Joseph had touched it before him. He was reaching for a scone, for cream and jam. He was hungry, as he always was. Beside him, Angus turned a biscuit over in his fingers, walked away with it without taking a bite. Ivy followed him with her eyes: was he heading for Bear? Often, she still saw the two of them, hunched over in conversation, their connection almost visible in the air, Marina flicking her gaze towards them. But Angus had found Hector, she saw: Bear was nowhere to be seen.

The day was windless, a perfect Sussex spring. Not quite as warm as Easter had been, but more delicate for it, a growing dome among suds, a transparency that asked to be broken. It was not right, Ivy felt, for Joseph's funeral to be as exquisite as this, such a clear image of the goodness of being alive. There was no morality in her feeling, only a cracking, as across ice on the pond in winter, a threat to the surface of things, a coming apart. She had the same sense when she listened to the news, these past few years, the mounting energy of the description of events in Germany persuasive, somehow, as though the news itself could create war.

She saw Genevieve in one of the groups closest to the pond, her legs stretched out on the grass. Again, this tearing sense of a holiday, of celebration. How to prevent a funeral from becoming a party? *Do not kiss people in hallways* could be a first rule, she thought. Let it not be sunny, let not the air be soaked with this spring languidness, the smell of flowers so strong it seemed to liquefy, to run along her blood.

Shall we walk?

It was Bear, at last, behind her at the tea table, lifting his hand against the sun, the light falling on his throat, catching his forearms. He said the words so lightly they sounded like nothing, a small game, tossing a ball between them. Something they might have done a thousand times before. Around her, Ivy felt the day becoming more beautiful, despite itself, betraying Joseph as she did, every leaf bright with mourning.

They were not alone until they reached the walled garden. They had to speak of trivial things before then, remaining a few feet apart. They carried themselves seriously, without rushing, as though not forgetting for a second that they were at a funeral. Bear kept his tie fully fastened, tucked within his jacket. Ivy still wore her Cuban heels: they dug into the soil.

The truth was that it was easy to forget – not Joseph, but the murmured chatter, the cherry tarts and sea creatures, Gilbert crying in the church and the studio, Marina's frozen poise. In the garden, every tree recalled another time, years of summer childhood before any of it happened, Joseph hanging from a branch until all the blood ran to his face;

looking like the jellyfish Ivy had seen on a beach once, puffed and pink. They passed the bushes where Angus had built them a camp one summer night, their shadows long on the grass, birds singing in the sun.

The walled garden was one of Ivy's favourite parts of Cressingdon: there was something futile and touching about the warm red walls, covered in vines, only play walls, not built for shelter, open to the sky. The rows of flowers, bobbing, their easy, ordered beauty. She looked up to the unmarked blue square: their allotment of time. So small, so regular. Bear cleared his throat, swung his arms; he had still not touched her.

I gave Joseph my book – before. He was reading it – I never heard what he thought—

Ivy saw Joseph in his sweat-scented room days before Easter, a clutch of crumpled papers against his bare chest. He had fallen asleep reading; something from university, she had probably thought. Something boring. She had closed the door, let him carry on, alone.

And now of course I'll never know and stupid of me anyway asking a boy – even a clever one. Just one of my notions. He had such a fresh mind, didn't he? He looked at Ivy briefly, as though not expecting an answer.

But he was always striving – like I am, constantly. A bloody pain.

He ran his fingers through his hair: they had stopped, awkwardly, on a narrow path between raised beds, so she was forced to face him directly as he spoke, as though they were in a play. She let herself look at the flowers. *Petunias*, she named them. *Begonias.* She wondered when he would kiss her.

That's what's so wonderful about you, Ivy, why I wanted—There isn't all that striving, for you, is there? You're just existing. You're simply yourself. So wonderfully yourself.

He reached for her hand, then, like a doctor in this one action that could give such medicine, such relief. She had been prescribed a pill, by a real doctor, the night Joseph disappeared, but it only stopped her, made her die, for a few hours. This – Bear's hand on hers – was something else: a sheet lifted above her on a summer day, floating back to her body.

You're so lucky, Ivy. It's beautiful, the way you are. So happy to paint and sing and write and never worry at all – you're only yourself—

He kissed her again, at last, and more firmly than before. He had not called her beautiful, not exactly. And his description of her made no match with her sense of her own life: it was like forcing the wrong piece of a jigsaw into a space. But – she felt the flowers, watching them. What was it Jesus said about lilies? *They neither toil nor spin . . .* Perhaps Bear could be right. Perhaps she could stop striving: could do everything for the pleasure of it, and give no importance to the future, to what she would become. The thought – when she gave herself to it – was like falling backwards into bed, the cool, delicious relief of it. She began kissing him harder; his hands were on her waist now, he was moving her back, until her dress met the wall: she felt the grain of the warm brick through the fabric, the bumps of it like rough skin against her. She could just stop trying, as he said: she could simply exist. She had a long, clear sense of her life as a single, translucent moment, unclouded by trial and ambition. She would drift; she would be.

Bear's hand was on her thigh, under her dress. Ivy had long held a fear that she would be found to be deformed, when someone finally touched her. How else would she know? But this was not like an examination: she had the sense of music again, of Bear as a musician, his practised fingers moving up now, under fabric, knowing, somehow, how to touch her. She closed her eyes, the sensations forming, blooms in the darkness, the shapes spreading out, growing upwards. She opened her eyes again: Bear was watching her, his bright eyes intent, serious. He was learning her, she realized, studying her as she shifted against him. It was a language, she saw now, the way he touched her.

This – the walled garden, the sky – was the world of objects, she could feel, but it was not empty. She filled it, becoming part of its beds, the gritted gravel of its paths. She could feel herself moving outwards, into the soft leaves against soil, the warm colours of petals in the buttered light, the deepening trails in the distance. She was taking her place in the world, not staying apart, as she usually did, but becoming everything, knowing it, accepting it. In her new life she would not fight to become herself: she would be all this, instead. She would be part of it all.

Don't stop, she whispered to Bear, and he did not stop. The colours merged and rose as she breathed against his shoulder, felt herself dissolving, meeting the sky. He laughed quietly: he kissed her neck, his mouth opening gently against her skin. *A blanket of kisses*, Ivy thought, the remembrance of Easter Day a sudden movement within her, a jolt back into time. Ivy opened her eyes and saw a squirrel leap on to a distant branch, saw the dive of it, the gap in the air of the jump, the world ablaze behind it. In the future, she knew she could never speak of the truth of this moment: her skirt pulled up against a wall at her brother's funeral, her breath slowing inside her. She would speak instead of seeing the squirrel in the air, the boldness of its body stretched onward against the sunset, as though it was changing, in that moment, taking off in flight.

They walked through the paths of hedges that now seemed friendly, gentle with the last light of the sky.

We'd better get back, Bear had said, taking his hand out of her underwear and resting it on her rear, as though all of this were natural, the way people acted every day, in walled gardens, with birds saluting the dusk. Ivy knew, distantly yet entirely, that it was wrong to have had such pleasure when Joseph was gone, and would never have pleasure again. But she could not *feel* in the wrong: she felt suspended, as she walked across the grass in her stockinged feet, her heels hanging from her hand. The air had become a new element, it seemed, and she was floating in it, hanging in time as she had promised herself, thinking of nothing.

When they saw Marina, striding across the lawn towards them, Ivy at first felt only a simple labelling: *There is my mother.* But then Bear dropped her hand, and she felt the roughness of the ground beneath her feet, a spiking stub of a thistle. The air was thin again: her body was so heavy, she realized, so dense and clumsy.

Ivy!

Marina was calling her name although she could see her, plain and only thirty feet away. She had no shoes on – this was not unusual – but was carrying a glass of red wine in her hand, the liquid forming waves as she walked, a small red sea. Marina very rarely drank: Ivy could not remember the last time she had. She was judgemental of those who got too drunk at their dinners, called them *slurring idiots.* But her son was dead. *Her son was dead.* Ivy felt a swell of sympathy for her mother, for herself: this could be part of her new life, she realized. She could be with people, in their suffering. She could be with Marina. She was always meaning to be kinder to her mother.

But as Marina got closer Ivy saw the pale pull of her face, the way her skin seemed barely to cover her features. She had seen this look as a child, once or twice. She had known to run away, to play in the garden as long as she could. It might mean a painting was coming, or a wave of rage, a darkness that lapped in the ceilings and floorboards, threatening to pull them all down. Once, it came before a long illness, a time when Marina was in bed for months, and Ivy was cared for by Angus and Joseph, fed bread and butter and never made to sleep. That was the spring when Anne came to Cressingdon, put the house in order, baking, singing in the kitchen. One day soon after, Marina simply got out of bed, started painting again.

Marina had put lipstick on this morning – another unusual thing – and it was smeared now, painted with the red wine above and below her lips, a second mouth. She didn't look at Bear, only at Ivy, the dark blue of her gaze so intense Ivy felt herself shudder.

Mother? Is everything all right?

Marina hated all the boys from the school, was always telling Ivy they were below her. And they were, Ivy saw now: all of them scruffy and drooping, weak-armed, smelling of their mothers' kitchens. And yet this did not please her either, Ivy saw: Marina was furious.

Ivy, may I speak with you, please?

Marina's teeth were gritted; Ivy thought of skulls, the way teeth stayed in them, pushed together, surviving skin and flesh and blood. Tiny bones. She thought of Joseph's: the chip in his front tooth, made when practising for her school's three-legged race. How they had bumbled together in the warm garden, the sharpness of dry grass on their forearms when they fell. Joseph had only laughed, but the chip was large. Ivy remembered the way it tilted his face, how Marina had held her fingertips to his mouth. *My beautiful boy.* There was talk of getting it fixed, of a tiny chip of china being glued in place. But it had never happened.

Come on now.

Marina took Ivy's bare arm in her hand: Ivy felt the length of her nails. She looked back at Bear, who was watching with a strange expression on his face, so far from her own confusion. Recognition, she could call it. Understanding, perhaps. When he spoke, his voice sounded distant, almost official.

I'll just – see if there's any food still going—

He turned quickly towards the garden group, his hands in his pockets. Marina had Ivy's arm more firmly now, the kind of grip that could leave a bruise. She steered Ivy into the house, up the stairs, all the time holding the glass of wine, never spilling a drop.

In her bedroom, Ivy felt relief, at first, at the sight of her familiar quilt on the bed, its regular pattern like days of childhood. She sat down; she wanted to live within their tiny florals, to lie back and think of the walled garden. She did not want to speak to her mother. But Marina was pacing by the window, her sleeves pulled up now, the hairs on her arms risen and visible in the low light. Behind her, distant fields soared up, a surge of earth. She seemed ten times bigger than Ivy, the tower from her infancy, the force that would scoop Ivy from the ground, hold her on a hip that moved impossibly fast through the house. It was like being on a train, or rather trains reminded Ivy of this, when she first rode them: of being carried by her mother.

Marina was looking at her: she was taking deep, long breaths, pursing her mouth as though about to whistle. On the wine glass, her hand twitched and shifted, finding the right position for speech. She exhaled again, kept her eyes against Ivy's.

Not him.

Her hand seemed to grip the glass tighter: Ivy looked from the glass to her mother, and back to the glass. It was clouded now, covered in fingerprints, more like a totem than something from the kitchen. She couldn't look away.

Anyone but him.

Ivy would remember not the image but the sound that the glass made as it was crushed, the high whine that seemed louder than the crack itself, the pressure built up before giving way. She would hear the noise everywhere, for her whole life: in the opening of a stuck window, an air-raid siren and the doodlebug that followed it, in an untuned organ, the starting cry of a baby in a crowded shop.

She would not remember the way the wine fell from the glass straight downwards, like a plug pulled, how it fell in that one glug, a mouthful, a round rush before the splash and the spill. It was the rug Anne had made her, soon after she came, Ivy calling out the colours as she picked away at her crochet needles. It was already loose, more of a scrap than a rug, and now it was ruined. Marina was on her knees, trying somehow to mop the rug with itself, folding it in a way that spread the wine to all its corners. She looked addled, disbelieving: Ivy had a glimpse, suddenly, of how she might look as an elderly woman, confused at the world.

I'll go, Mother. Stop – I'll do it. Leave it alone.

Ivy went downstairs; she was taken aback to see that people were still there, that the funeral was, in some sense, continuing. Anne had cleared away the luncheon food, and in its place there were small toasts, spread with something beige – probably fish paste – and round biscuits topped with cheese. Genevieve and Hector were talking with Angus, who looked up as Ivy passed to the kitchen. She was surprised to see Frances still there, talking to Gilbert now; he looked crumpled, even more worn out than before, but Frances seemed to have gained some new light, an ease in her movements. She had been drinking, Ivy thought, was something closer to the girl who had visited at Easter, a girl who was joyful even without drink. Bear was nowhere to be seen.

In the kitchen, Anne was bent over the sink, again, her arms pink raw in the way they always got when she washed up, her hair catching the light from the bulb above her head. They had only had electricity for a few years and Ivy still found it strange, the luminescent globes that hung, bulbous, that never flickered in the wind. When she was a child, Anne always followed her when she carried a candle to bed.

You'll set the place alight, Jesus Mary and Joseph. Say your prayers now.

And Ivy would kneel by the bed, her lips moving against her pressed palms, as though her mouth were itself a small god, with its own rituals. She had heard the sounds of the house: Joseph with a friend in the garden, the low moan of the gramophone in the studio. Behind her closed eyes, there was nothing, a paused calm. When Marina found out about the praying, she forbade it: afterwards, there was only a silence after Anne walked her to bed, a space where the prayers had been. *Get into bed now,* Anne would say, and lean down and kiss her once on the forehead, so lightly it felt like a dusting of flour, the edge of a wing.

Can I fill a bowl? Ivy asked now, moving to the sink. She placed a hand on Anne's arm, felt the complex warmth of it: her body had always felt like a country to her, a land with unknown dimensions, the thick straps of her brassiere, the visible line of undergarments under her skirts. Marina had a straight, boyish body, but Anne was like a woman in a painting: there was so much of her. As a child, Ivy felt that Anne's soul was larger, too, spread through her person, resting in the high plains of her cheeks, the round peaks of her shoulders. When she was very small, Ivy had liked to curl into her lap and remain there as long as Anne would let her, feel the protection of her softness like a castle.

What's happened now? Anne said, filling the bowl for her, fetching a piece of cotton that she turned under the tap. Ivy wondered what had already been spilt, turned over, how much mess and embarrassment she had missed.

Mother spilt some wine. Ivy rolled her eyes in what she hoped was a grown-up, ironic way. She wanted to smile with Anne about Marina, as they did sometimes. But Anne only frowned.

Wine?

Ivy nodded, looking down. She would not mention Bear, though she had some strange impulse to, even now feeling the way he had touched her, as though she was the only thing on the earth. She wondered if he had gone to the station already: she imagined him on the train to London, flying through a navy field, the stars like a Van Gogh, swirled into the sky.

Anne looked hard at Ivy: her eyes were filmed, Ivy realized, reflective as the pond.

I know, with Joseph and all – this day – but, Ivy. He's so very much older than you.

In her whole life, Ivy had so rarely felt Anne and Marina united against her: it was a force, she saw now, a tower of understanding that she could barely see beyond, Anne's face clear and steady, her fair hair scraped back in a bun, her cheeks pink in the steam from the sink. Ivy took the bowl and cloth, not speaking. She turned away so Anne could not see the mottling of her face, the way it was folding into itself, the tears she swallowed down.

She walked through the hallway where Bear had kissed

her: it was another planet now, lit electrically, full of shadows that rose and shifted. Here was Joseph running as a child, his socks skidding against the wood. And there was Gilbert leaving one day for the last time, the bulk of his suitcase against his leg. And here was the spot, against the wall, where Bear had so gently put his lips against hers: she felt again the silk of them, shaking away the images of Anne's face, Marina's face, layering and looping against her.

She tightened her fists against her dress, readying herself for her mother in a rage, for more than this. *She has lost her son.* Hector said this to Ivy in the first few days after it happened: he was rushing out of Marina's bedroom, having failed to convince Aunt Genevieve to come home with him. Ivy had asked him how Marina was, and he turned to look at her, as though this was no question at all.

Ivy was surprised by how long Aunt Genevieve stayed after Joseph died, how she was able to exist in the damp, saturated air of Marina's bedroom. Genevieve hated confrontation: she had been known, when Angus and Joseph began a spat at the table, to stand up and leave. But to lie with Marina was only to confront silence, and darkness. It was to sit together and watch a black wave rise at the window, as though they lived on the beach of a sea of oblivion. Which, Ivy supposed, they did.

Genevieve managed what Ivy had not: she comforted Marina. Ivy saw it, carrying a bowl of soup in one afternoon, saw the two sisters lying as she had lain with her mother when she was very small: with mouths open and close to each other, as though sharing the same breath.

Now, on the landing, everything was quiet: Ivy stood still beside a gilt frame, an early work of Marina's blazing within it: the detail of a fireplace, heavy layers of paint, the world of objects luminous here, seeming to shine with unknown hope. To live in this house was to encounter pieces of her mother everywhere: from early childhood, Ivy had been reminded, over and over, of parts of Marina that she could not access, that could only be seen here, in oils, in weeks of old work.

She passed a print of Zurbarán's *St Francis in Ecstasy*, owned by Gilbert and never removed, for some reason, though Marina claimed to hate it. She detested religion as she did nothing else in the world: everything else could be embraced, passionately or at least with good humour. Even horror and death and destruction fed art. But not God: religion was the opposite of art, she had told Ivy once, when Ivy had expressed fascination for Joan of Arc. *It is the end of exploration.* Marina had even suggested they bury Joseph's coffin in the woodland at the bottom of the garden. *Like pagans*, she had said. *Why not?* But Gilbert wouldn't have it: he insisted – using what authority he had left – on a church funeral. He had only ever insisted once before, that Joseph go to what he called a *proper school*, where he himself had been. He had not insisted that Ivy do anything. Ivy had attended Mrs Morpeth's Academy, where she put on plays and sewed costumes and was woken from bed while it was still dark to go on a boat ride. She could barely do a simple sum.

It was Gilbert who had given her a book of the saints' lives, a gift from his mother, Grandmother Emily, a Catholic convert, a *dreadfully religious* woman, as he put it, prone to shrines in the garden, a dangle of rosary beads from her wrist. Ivy could follow her grandmother's jagged underlines, her spidery annotations in the margins. *Very brave*, Emily had written beside a description of a saint who kept a knife in his pocket, who plunged it into himself rather than deny Christ. *Disgusting*, she had thought St Lucy, who had her eyes gouged out and carried them on a plate. Ivy read the accounts over and over, marvelling at a dedication she had only ever seen – in her own home – for art, for paintings that would hang on the wall. But this was passion, it seemed to Ivy; a fiery, mysterious love she could not begin to understand. Religion was so much bloodier in the olden days: so much more full of bodies and smell and adventure, a far cry from Reverend Giles and the stale air of his sermons. Perhaps even Marina would have liked it more, then.

In the bedroom, Marina had not moved. The wine seemed ancient now, grown into the rug naturally, like moss. It seemed impossible that Ivy would be able to wash it away with the little cloth she carried, the shaking bowl of water. But they tried: Marina helped, pulling the rug taut while Ivy dipped the cloth and scrubbed, dipped it again. For a few minutes, they didn't speak: the stain persisted. It spread, weakened until the rug was a new colour, and it seemed that they had finished.

There was a knock at the door. Anne, her apron finally off, watching Ivy and Marina on the floor.

It's getting late— Shall I tell them to go home?

Marina seemed not to hear at first, sitting back on her heels, one hand still on the damp rug. But then a frown lowered her features, her head flicking to Anne, her mouth opening in a snap.

Tell them to go home? Who do you think you are, Anne? Close that damned door behind you—

Marina had never, in Ivy's presence, spoken to Anne like this. She could be curt, but she was always polite. She had never sworn at her, never used her name in that way. And still Anne did not leave: she stood by the door, paused, uncertain. Ivy began to feel the room undulate, the fabrics of things coming apart. The world of objects was so easily disturbed, she saw now, the bed blurring into the floor-boards, the wardrobe melting with the carpet. Ivy felt sure that something would happen: Anne would speak back, perhaps there could even be an argument. But Anne only nodded, closing the door gently behind her. Marina looked at the rug, her eyes distant.

Rupert – Bear – was there when you were born, you know. He held you.

Ivy had heard stories of the day she was born: 1918, the earth frozen, the land white, the first Christmas of peace. Marina gave birth in her bedroom, the doctor moving in and out, asking her to lift her legs, to lower them. Joseph – a tiny child – jumped in the hallway, shouting until he was quietened. Angus and Gilbert stood with him – and Bear, it seemed now. Ivy tried to imagine the raffish figure she'd seen in photos, standing at the doorway, his hairline lower, his jaw sharper, all of them so young, grouped in concern.

Said how beautiful you were.

Marina had the cloth: she squeezed it into the bowl, the pink water running over her fingers. She took her time, no longer cleaning but playing, it seemed, laying the cloth against her palm and pushing it off again, letting it fall back, limp in the water. She had told Ivy of the hours after she was born, how Angus and Gilbert took Joseph for a walk in the freezing air, how she felt that she and Ivy were the only people in the world. How quiet it was, and then: the sound of carol singers, somehow, across the fields.

Marina reached for her hand: it was wet and sliding, but Ivy held on. She felt their old touch, present somewhere below the numb press of their hands, as though the past were inside their bodies, under their skin.

He said— Marina laughed quickly, bitterly. Ivy dropped her hand.

He said: What if I marry her? Marina closed her eyes. She

began speaking quietly, as though to herself, in a sing-song, lilting imitation.

Could I marry her? Would it be strange? She is such a perfect little thing.

At that moment her mother's speech was not a revelation but its opposite: a contortion, an aberration. Ivy could feel herself nodding her head, biting her lip; such tiny, pointless movements. She folded her arms across herself, as though for protection.

You like him, don't you? You poor thing. Marina's tone was slanted, almost mocking: Ivy saw how she could change Bear's touches into something pitiful, sordid. She almost wondered at it: such power of transformation.

Marina looked at Ivy: her eyes were bloodshot, barely focusing. Ivy saw it clearly now, as though in a cinema: the crowd around the child-bed, her own self: small and crooked against her mother's arm. The room was warmly lit, in her imagination: it was burnished, golden. And Bear, making a plan, even then. Marina took one deep breath, let it out with another flow of words, these coming almost casually at first, as though an afterthought.

Joseph wouldn't have liked it, you know, Ivy. He always thought – he always knew he was too old for you. Not right for you.

The four last words were said through narrowed teeth, the red stain around Marina's lips the new edge of her mouth. Ivy wiped her hands on her dress. Around her, the bedroom was no longer a sanctuary: her bedspread looked different, the squares now a dizzying maze, a labyrinth she had no hope of understanding. Marina was squeezing the water again, her knuckles bare bones in the lamplight. Ivy knew she should do something, lift her mother, gentle her, take her to bed. *She has lost her son.* But she couldn't – she didn't. She moved towards the door, was somehow amazed to find that she could open it easily, that her mother said nothing. She left.

Ivy, darling! Aunt Genevieve called to her from a low sofa, a clear drink in her hand. She held her niece's hand in that desperate way older women did, squeezing, as though they could pass wisdom by osmosis, make the younger woman see all she had before her.

Your hands are so cold! Where have you been?

Helping Mother. Ivy sat close to Genevieve, felt the warmth of her, smelt the alcohol on her breath, a sweet echo of Bear's earlier that day. Across the smoke of the room Ivy could see Hector, his round glasses perched low on his nose. He was speaking to Frances in an uninterrupted stream, his hands making outlines in the air. Frances looked like she was sliding down the night, as though she would soon finally give up, claim a headache, call a taxi. Ivy knew she should rescue her, but she was so tired. She wanted to put her head in Genevieve's lap, like she used to. She wanted her aunt's cool hands on her forehead. But Genevieve was asking her questions:

And what will you do, darling? After – all this. Mummy said you were writing now?

Ivy wanted to be honest, suddenly. She could see no reason for pretence. She thought of the walled garden, of the relief of not striving, any more. Of being who Bear said she was.

I don't know, Genevieve. I don't think I have any talent, for anything. Maybe – maybe I'll get married.

Married! But you're so young. What about all your plans? I know you wanted to travel, perhaps with a theatre group, didn't you say. Or dance?

Ivy nodded, as though acknowledging the plans of a small child, things she had asked for on long-ago birthdays.

I did say that, I suppose.

Genevieve gripped her hand again.

I know this is all so – awful. But we mustn't give up, must we? We must carry on. Like we did in the war. And with another war on the cards—

Ivy nodded, dumbly. She studied the room again, squinting. Hector was refilling his pipe over the card table. Frances had escaped, was hovering beside the food, which was dismantled again, picked over by the invisible crowd. Ivy watched Frances place a prawn in her mouth, and then another, and another, as though they were sweets, and she was at a circus. Angus was nowhere to be seen. Bear must have left, she realized, when she was with Marina. He must have simply driven away. The wanting had changed now, she found. The pulse was gone; she wanted him like she wanted sleep, at the end of a long day. Or a piece of bread, when she was hungry.

Frances walked over to them, a near-empty champagne flute tipping in her hand. She sat down next to Ivy; there was something gentle in her, almost lazy, without expectation. Genevieve carried on—

. . . *and please let me know if there's anything I can do. You could come and stay with Hector and me for a while, if that would suit. You know how much space we have.*

Ivy thought of Genevieve's house, so different from Cressingdon; *Walnut Corner*, they called it, quiet rooms with pulled-back curtains covered in patterns, falling leaves that turned to deer, berries to rings. Bess, the uniformed maid who always made Ivy feel that she was standing in the wrong place. Genevieve's door was shut all morning, the volume of the house turned down to the hum of her mind, Hector's whispered insistence that *she's writing*. When she was younger, Ivy could not run in that house, or sing. She spent whole days pretending she was a pirate, or an invisible fairy, pressed against the walls.

Aunt Genevieve had *moods*, as she called them, just as Marina did. They got it from their father, Marina said once, a Victorian gentleman who was so anxious he made everyone recite every penny they'd spent that day at supper. But Ivy had never seen Genevieve rip a canvas in two with her bare hands. She had never even heard Genevieve raise her voice. *No children*, she had heard Marina say, almost spitting the words. *All the time in the world. And Hector waiting on her every bloody need.* Marina would have been more successful by now, Ivy had understood – as successful as Genevieve, as Angus – had she and Joseph not existed at all. *Such a stellar family*, Ivy's teachers at school had always said. *So bohemian! It must be wonderful.* And Ivy had agreed: there was nothing else she could say.

There was a noise from upstairs, a kind of rolling knock, and then a yell. The room around Ivy seemed to shift sideways, a way of listening while continuing to talk, to sip drinks, eat a piece of congealed cheese on a biscuit. Aunt Genevieve frowned at Ivy, as if Ivy had made the noise herself. Frances arranged herself, folding her skirts over her knees, as though remembering where she was. She too tilted her head to one side. Then as quickly as the listening had begun it ended: it was easy to dismiss a single noise.

Would you get me another drink, dear? Aunt Genevieve was closing her eyes: Ivy wondered how long this funeral could continue for, if they had slipped into some mistake in time, that they might be trapped here, speaking of nothing, mourning Joseph, for ever. She could sit with Frances until the end of their lives, she realized, and talk of nothing but her brother. They would tell stories over and over, the same stories gaining meaning by repetition; the time Joseph had attempted to bake a cake and the whole thing was liquid, how lit up his face was regardless, how proud. The time he had upset a punt and plunged himself and Frances into a freezing, springtime river. Perhaps this last story would silence them, but then surely they would begin again.

The shouts were like a normal, household-sounding call at first, her own name, called a thousand times before up and down the stairs.

Ivy!

The guests were fully silent now: they turned to watch as Ivy stood up.

Ivy!

The voice was different on the second call: it was beginning to break, the volume making scratches in the sound, an audible scraping of the throat.

Ivy!

This one collapsed into a sob: the room was alarmed now, Ivy thought, or perhaps that was only her, palms turned silken, heart so present and loud within her. Marina.

There was a movement from the garden, a shifting from complete stillness, almost as though a statue had moved again, turned from stone to flesh. She saw Angus, the small glow of a cigarette at his lips, and behind him, a shadow, then a flick of fairness catching the light. Bear. He had not left! He was there, smoking, with Angus; perhaps he had been with him all this time. She saw both men turn towards the sound from the bedroom, Angus lifting a hand to his hair, exchanging a look with Bear that was lost to the dark. Under his foot, Angus extinguished his cigarette, moved towards the house. But Bear remained, alone, looking towards the window blankly before seeming to see, before turning – yes – *yes* – towards her. Ivy stood up. She made her way towards the door, imagining the smooth panel of her back speaking of her dutiful daughterliness, her response to her mother that was not quick, but was there nonetheless. They would think her solicitous, kindly, to be attending to Marina along with Angus, presenting her with a sip of water, a cool hand on her forehead. But once she was in the hall-way, then at the side door, nobody could see her. Nobody could judge the daughter who turned, not towards her mother but to the garden, to the shape she could still see outlined against the trees. Bear, his head dipped as though listening to some distant noise, waiting for her.

This time, they moved quickly, running towards the trees as towards a rushing ocean, the sound of the leaves soft, tidal in the darkness. She did not want them to be seen by Angus, or worse, by Marina, from the window. Did not want to be spotted by Anne or Genevieve or Hector or even Frances like this: her dress whipped around her body, her hand hold-ing Bear's like a tether, one boat tied to the other. His objections were weak, short-lived, and now he was with her, entirely, their bodies both solid and young-seeming, both mature and youthful enough to run like this, holding hands, barely out of breath.

The calls of her name had stopped but still seemed to ring around Ivy, sound travelling through her body like the aftermath of a bell, chiming with the race of her heartbeat. She had never been scared of the dark; she preferred it, in fact. As a child, during games of hide-and-seek, she was always the one willing to go into the garden, luring people reluctantly from the warmth and light of the house. She loved to wait, crouched safe in the bushes, unseen, while everyone else called her name. She liked to hear the way their voices became more and more frantic, the way they lengthened the last syllable like a banshee call, tiring or perhaps frightened: of losing her, or of the dark itself. Even when she was eleven or twelve she would suggest the game, and sometimes Joseph would agree, leaping from his chair unexpectedly, making her run.

Now, she threw her head back to the house, its lights a ship on the black sea of the lawn. In the darkness, the world of objects was sunken, blurred: she could not distinguish between the pond and grass until they were beside them, at risk of tripping as her foot struck a rock. She let out a cry, and Bear stopped: he turned.

Are you all right? Look, why are we—

But she kissed him: took his mouth in her own to stop him speaking, his hands around her waist, like tying her hair in a ribbon; such ease; she had heard stories about him, flutters of talk through open doors. *Hundreds of lovers.* She imagined the hundreds, a great army of the naked and beautiful, parading through the streets of London. She thought of

Bear as a younger man, striding down a wide street, imagined the way the world felt to him: open, pulsing, as though the whole city were a woman, asking for his attention. It was like telepathy, the way he had moved his fingers in exactly the way she wanted him to. But it was different to before, in the walled garden; it felt, suddenly, that they were moving towards something together, running as though to a cliff, to fall through perfect, clear air.

Bear became concentrated, almost mathematical, frowning as he unbuttoned his trousers, his whole form loosening as he assumed what she saw was his natural position, completely himself, his eyes closed, his skin perfectly smooth. So this was it: so different from kissing, even from being touched, a huge upheaval, as though the territory of herself was being mapped at last, its borders redrawn. She tried to give herself to it; she tried to stop thinking. But the thoughts only came faster: the bowl, the pink water running over Marina's fingers, the rug with its new ochre colour, like an old bloodstain. Perhaps, Ivy thought now, Marina did not want her daughter to love anyone but her. She thought of her mother's face, earlier that evening, the features made alien with disgust. *You poor thing.*

Ivy shook herself, returned to sensation, Bear's face damp against hers, his breathing full of the desire she had so often imagined but never heard, its expression laced with unreality as it built in force, Bear's self within her, around her, through her. And where was she? Lost in it, it seemed, as Bear called

out into the darkness, something painful in the sound, something *funereal*, Ivy could not help thinking, as he kissed her
forehead, his breathing slowing, his hands still around her.
Ivy felt only stillness, then a void, an absence of meaning that
grew, thickened.

Joseph wouldn't like it.

And there it was: there he was. Joseph, stepping into the
river that night, his long back shining, his hair a seal slick as
he rose up, gasping, spitting.

Come in!

Then: his last voice, his call to her simply an accompani-
ment, at that moment, to the light that branched and pulsed
above her, a new horizon, dazzling.

Ivy.

It was Bear – not Joseph – gentle now, stroking her face
with his fingertips.

Ivy? I hope you are – I hope that was—

He was stumbling now, all of a sudden, almost boyish. Con-
cerned, for her, or for his own performance, she wasn't sure.
But she had nothing in her for reassurance, for stroking his hair
or meeting his hands with her own. She wanted coolness, she
found. Immersion. She wanted this as clearly as she had wanted
Bear, just hours ago, this wanting of him its own lesson. She
knew what it was to want something, now. To take it.

She moved away, their tangled flesh and fabric parting, her
feet bare on the earth again, a burning inside her. She stood
up, rearranged her clothes, not looking at Bear but feeling his

eyes upon her, the question as he opened his mouth. But before he could speak she had left, breaking into a run as she passed through the orchard, hearing Bear beginning to call after her, his voice stuttering into the night, hitting the trees, caught in the brambles. But Ivy didn't stop: she went on, faster now, her legs becoming scratched, getting to where the woods were dense, left to their own unruliness, their branches enmeshed, becoming one. She stumbled against a fallen tree in the near-darkness, its round strength hitting her knees. She kept going.

Ivy came to where the trees thinned, where there was a pathway, a piece of rope from a leftover swing. She had gone this way with Joseph on Easter night, him bounding ahead, touching the frayed rope and laughing. *It never worked properly*, he'd said. *We kept bumping the other trees.* She remembered the sight of the river opening up to them, as it did now, always a surprise, the rush and wideness of it, so much fiercer than she imagined, every time.

At Easter the moon had not been as full: tonight the river looked white, a flowing milky softness. Ivy sat on the bank, feeling her toes moving into the soft mud at its edges. She only lowered her feet in, to the ankles: the river felt familiar, gently wet, less cold than she had expected.

She could see that the grass was flattened in places: *from Easter*, she thought, imagining Joseph's large shoes, his stumble as they undressed. Or from the search party: men with lanterns, women with hands cupped around their mouths, calling.

Bear's book is a load of nonsense, honestly. I can't bear to tell him.

Joseph had stood on one leg to pull a sock off, his large loose body jumping a little as he did so, the skin soft and stippled, covered in freckles.

Might get Angus to do it – he could break it with a kiss.

Ivy had leant down and splashed him, when he said that. Now, she imagined it: Angus with his hands around Bear's face. A long kiss. It felt as though, of all of them, Angus was the only one capable of having a true love affair. She could picture the two men in golden fields in the summer, the world more beautiful, unravaged. She could see their bare chests, the way they turned to each other.

Now, she knew what Bear's kisses felt like. She knew how expert he was, how seductive. She saw how this knowledge lay alongside her knowledge of Angus: of his painting, his hair in his eyes. She looked at the moon, as though for help: yet there was only Easter again, in the trees and the grass, in every smell, in the lick of the current around her ankles, the slow drag of the water away from her. Without undressing, she pushed her feet further and further into the river: the water was so soft it hardly felt cold at all. Still, she did not undress, did not even think of undressing: she let her body slide in as a boat slides, pushed down a bank. There was something inevitable in it, her legs, her back, her head moving into the water, the world green-black around her. It was selfish, she knew, to go into the water, on this day of all days. But the day was already broken: it had been broken from the beginning.

She swam out, the cloth of her dress widening, the weeds thick around her legs, broad tongues lapping; she felt sleepy, safe, as though the water were the blankets her mother wrapped her in at bedtime, singing those strange, slow songs, lowering Ivy into the dark. She saw how everything could disappear so quickly, that the house – all its china and art-work and dresses – would one day be floating itself, when the seas closed over the land, when the whole world was water. No one would even see the blurred paint that Marina and Angus spent so many hours layering and perfecting. Everything would be floating: everything would be gone.

She sank beneath, just for a second, then for a few seconds more. A dark presence rushed towards her, a sense like the darkness when she closed her eyes at night – that interior quiet, that continual breathing – but deepened, darkened still further by fathoms of water. She resurfaced, took a breath, but the water was stronger, the wrap of the vines, the hands of the current across her. She sank again. The plunging, the soft welcome of nothing, her life gone, the world gone, navy, spreading: then a warmth began. It was born, it seemed, from nowhere, growing like a tiny dawn across the black. She sensed the world of objects give way, gently, and here was what remained: an infinite pale softness, an ocean of being. Joseph was there, she knew, somewhere. He was reaching for her.

Ivy. Ivy.

Marina had named her, for the Christmas plant, the vines that wrapped around the window as they lay there, in winter silence, as the baby opened her mouth to an O.

Ivy.

Someone was saying her name again, over and over, exhausting its noises, turning it to nonsense. She was being pulled, she could feel, taken from the blank sky, the new dawn. She was being taken away.

A smell of bleach, and perfume. The white of a plain hospital wall, electrically lit. Wall and bed and chair, singular and formed beside her. And a face. A woman in a blue cap, who leant over so close Ivy could smell not only perfume but more intimate things, her perspiring and her breath, the yeasty earthiness of it.

Another face: Marina, further away, only a movement and a colour, then a voice.

Darling? Are you there? She leant forward then, and held one of Ivy's hands in her own. The gentlest smear of lipstick was visible on her cheek. A smell of vomit, distant or close. Disinfectant. The body and its erasing.

Nurse! She's awake. Can you fetch the doctor?

Marina's hands were cold and thin, a hard pressing. Ivy tried to move but her mother was strong: she had her tightly. Angus was there too, she saw now, at Marina's side as always, his face impassive.

Bear! He rescued you! You were – almost dead, darling. He brought you to life.

Marina was crying, Ivy could see, in that peculiar way she did, no change to her mouth or the expression of her eyes, only a rolling of water down her cheeks, a leaking of feeling. Ivy imagined it, and then seemed to remember, a distant fragment, a piece of flotsam coming closer on the water. Bear's arms around her, his head against hers. Can it have been so romantic as this? She had vomited, no doubt. Soiled herself. But now she was clean, and in a hospital bed: perhaps she could stay here for ever, she thought. People could be faces, arriving and leaving. She could do nothing.

The doctor came; he proclaimed her a miracle.

Gave us quite a scare! You were gone, we think – for a moment there.

The doctor chuckled; he was young and handsome. Ivy saw Marina and Angus watching him, closely, following his hands as they performed their tests. Ivy passed all of them, without meaning to: she had not even tried.

★

At some point later – an hour, or a minute, Ivy could not tell – Bear arrived, sitting by the bed, his hands clasped as though he was praying, his knees apart. He looked serious, older than she had ever seen him, the bare patch on the top of his head showing as he bent down, a gleaming, pointed egg.

Are you all right, old thing?

She nodded. She thanked him. Bear was shifting in his seat, sliding one hand against the other in a skating movement, its pace increasing as he began to speak.

Ivy – seeing you, like that. I want to always – keep you safe, to protect you. Would you ever consider—

Ivy looked at the ceiling: it had hurt, to keep her neck turned for so long. She watched the shadow of trees on the hospital wall, thrown into contrast by moonlight. There was a dance, there, she began to notice, a play that reminded her of the light she had seen at Easter. The beauty of it: she knows it must have been exceptional, to have prevented her from hearing, from knowing what was happening to her brother. But it was gone. Even in the water, that clear peace she had felt: it seemed to exist only on the other side of life, only in death itself. *She lost her brother*, she heard one of the nurses mumbling to another: from the corner of her eye she had seen the nurses' slow nod, as though it explained everything.

Now, Ivy turned to Bear, her eyes filling freely. She was so moved, she would say later. She was so touched by Bear's love, by his need to protect her. But the truth was, she realized it no longer mattered what she did. She could be with Bear or not be with Bear: it was all the same. The world that she could see was a play world, where one action meant the same as another. She could be a girlfriend, a wife, even. She could work, travel, have children: none of it made any difference. If she were married, at least she would be free from any expectation, any pretence of ambition. All the paintings in the world were insubstantial, in a sense, compared to this: a solid husband, a solid life. Something even Marina had not managed.

Dear Bear, she said, the tears spilling over now, rolling on to her lips, a great relief in letting them fall. *Of course. I would love nothing else.*

DAY THREE

April 1944

THEY HAD NOT slept well for years. There had been bombs, and a baby, and then babies and bombs together, explosions of fire and screaming in the night, the two of them standing and rocking, watching the flashes, holding infants to their chests. Ivy had been surprised at Bear, at the calm way he had handled their first daughter, his enthusiasm for nappies and milk, for mashing potato to a pulp. He did not mind when one daughter and then the next lifted their spoon and threw the food in his face, at the wall, even when it was their last potato, even when he had grown it himself, delivered it from the soil to his hands.

That morning he was first to get up when the noises began from the children's room, the soft gabble of four-year-old Artemis, the sharp cries of her sister, Baby. None of them had taken to the baby's real name – Pansy – and so she seemed, at two, destined to remain Baby, even when she was grown and had babies of her own. Ivy lay in bed, turned over on her side, her eyes closed in a picture of sleep. She heard Bear pulling on his clothes, opening the door with a creak, could feel him lift Baby from her cot, rest the child on his hip. *Come on, Artemis,* she heard him saying. *Let's get breakfast.* She had long since stopped being surprised by the sight of Bear – now slightly more stooped, and with a paunch – as father to such young children. It was only when she saw other fathers that she noticed how upright they were, how abundant their hair, the tightness of their skin.

Downstairs, she could hear the plates sliding out, tin cups being banged against their wooden table. Baby was getting teeth and liked to chew on a spoon all day, to gurn and whine and dribble until at night she turned puce and began to wail in agony. All the remedies – or placebos – that had worked for Artemis proved futile for Baby; they were failing, Ivy sometimes felt, letting her fall into pain like that, over and over again. She turned on to her back, opened her eyes to the grey squares of sky visible from the windows, watched the innocent clouds move across from one pane to the next. She saw the way the clouds were breaking, as the days seemed to, as lack of sleep frayed the air, made every moment of family life appear fragile, on the cusp of collapse.

And this was not even to think of the war: Ivy knew how it had shaped them, always knowing of danger; she knew that the very stuff of their children's bodies was built from war, Artemis born in London with sirens and searchlights surrounding her. She remembered cradling the tiny child, Bear manic with anxiety and exultation. They had lain close that night, the three of them in one bed, and Ivy felt that they were blessed, protected: there was no nearby raid, no shaking of the walls. But just weeks later, Ivy was pushing Artemis in her pram and the park exploded, reality shattering, the bodies of trees coming apart in the blue sky, the world fragmenting, flying into space. An undiscovered bomb, it was said afterwards. It was lucky, they said, that no children were on the playground. For weeks, Ivy heard it: that high ring in her ears.

After that, Bear demanded that they leave, move to the country. He would still have to return to London for his desk job at the BBC, but it would be safer, he insisted. They would be happy. He found a slanting cottage to rent in the middle of muddy fields, its windowpanes painted royal blue. Ivy had the sense that it was sinking into the earth, that the cracks in its ceiling were opening further every day, letting in a darkness that lived in the soil, that blew through the foundations. The cottage was only a mile away from Cressingdon, the bigger house just visible from the upper windows. *Too near Mother*, Ivy had told Bear. *Too near Angus.* But Bear insisted: she would need family. She would be grateful. And it was true that Artemis adored going to her grandmother's house, being allowed to cover canvas scraps with paint, run naked across the lawn. There was that terrible time last year when Bear's back had given in: Ivy had gone for their rations and returned to find Artemis trapped in the clothes horse, Bear paralysed, unable to help her. Ivy was six months pregnant: she had sat and cried, with Artemis sobbing on her knee. Marina had come eventually, with Anne, after Ivy had failed to appear for tea as arranged. Marina bathed Artemis and sang her strange songs; Anne made soup.

This is how life happens, Ivy realized, like a crowd of things and houses and people pushed by a tidal wave, moving towards her, over her. Life took place, and she was within it, but there seemed to be no control, no choice. She had been expecting something different; she had decided, that day in hospital, that none of her choices mattered. But she had expected choices, nonetheless. She had not gone to university, that was hardly a surprise. But she did not paint, or write, or dance or sing, these days. Bear had never published his new book; they had children, that was all, and their lives had narrowed, without them noticing, to this conventional shape: they had become just like everyone else.

Ivy got out of bed and put on the nearest clothes, a patched shirt, an old dress of Marina's. She had no interest in clothes now, except for purest function: she thought only of warmth, and durability, for them all. She had forgotten about elegance, the sense of walking into a room and being looked at. During their brief courtship, Bear had taken her to restaurants where she had experienced the small thrill of a room's gaze settling on her face, her body, like sunlight. There was an oyster place they used to go, where Bear seemed to expect her to be embarrassed by the wet folds of the creatures, where he snapped his fingers at the waiters, insisted on a better table.

There was a pleasurable resignation, Ivy had found, in being on his arm, being led along the street. Is this part of why women love men? she wondered now. Because they can lead them like this? She did not have to get lost, or found, she did not have to think about where she was going at all. She was led along like a kind of dog, or like a sprite, her feet hardly touching the ground. She remembered one night, when they went to the cinema after dinner, her body remaining untethered, floating through the darkness as through outer space. She was too full, of crustaceans and wine, the whole mixture threatening to brim over inside her.

Next to her, Bear had swung one leg over another, rested one hand on hers, as though it was nothing. He had begun to rub, to loop over her thumb, down into the crevice where it joined her forefinger, up and down over and again, his eyes glassy, fixed on the film. Ivy had felt the chair soften under her, the theatre seeming to press around them until there was only the sensation, her whole body giving way.

These were the pleasures of love, it seemed: to be seen, and to be touched. To give way to the wave of life, let it carry her. Before she had children, Ivy had counted her life in her heart, weighed every experience for its gravity: she found each one light, wispy, liable to be blown away. Now, occasionally – when pushing the pram down the lane, the sky pinking over the hills – the fabric of the air seemed to thicken, to vibrate with significance. If she were a poet she would have written about it: the sense of the earth holding its breath, the planet turning with possibility, even in the midst of war.

It had been Bear's idea, to ask Reverend Giles for help.

She would not have thought of approaching him; that hunched, timid figure, who seemed to have less sense of the divinity of existence than the average man. But he had books, so many books: on biblical history, theological philosophy, mystical doctrine. He recommended a few things, but mostly was happy to leave Ivy alone in his study, let her find the things that interested her. Ivy searched in the books for references to lights in the sky, even for that sense she had, pushing the pram: the opening of the world. There was nothing. Then one day, in a small, dusty hardback, she read of a humble monk, Brother Lawrence, who thought of God at all times, who practised this thinking until his very life seemed to hum with the divine, a presence of warmth that the monk could turn to, regard as a friend. The monk was a pot-washer in a medieval monastery, and Ivy reflected that her life was not so different: if he could do it, and delight in his drudgery, in the sameness of his days, then so could she. But so far, God had proved elusive, distant, even absent. Ivy feared that she had made a mistake, in comparing herself to a monk. In this, as in all things, she seemed to lack talent.

God's absence is part of His essential being, Reverend Giles had told her, when Ivy described her struggle, but she could not for the life of her understand this explanation. Some theological grounding had passed her by: perhaps, she reflected occasionally, she had inherited a basic atheism from Marina, just as she had inherited her eyes.

She went down the stairs, hearing the first pained wail

from Baby, Artemis's voice slicing across it, high with questions. *What do sheeps eat, Daddy?* Ivy opened the door and saw her daughter kneeling on a chair, curls of hair tucked behind her ears: Artemis held a spoon of porridge above her bowl, tipped the handle and let it slide back again to the quivering pile, before taking another spoonful.

Grass, darling. Bear fetched a cloth for Baby's mouth, which was red-raw with dribble. *Good morning, Mummy.* Recently, he had started calling her this: *Mummy*, and himself *Daddy* in the third person. Ivy experienced a small lifting each time he said it, a feeling more like dizziness than elation, a sense of rising above herself. Now, Artemis echoed him: *Good Mummy.* Ivy kissed each of them, then took her place at the stove, so like Anne's had always been: mopping and stirring, filling a kettle for more tea. On the table were the flowers she and the girls picked a week ago, pathetic now in their faded drooping, the crinkle of their stems.

Where do we go when we die? Artemis asked now, turning her spoon in the air. Lately, Artemis had been fascinated with death. *When will I die?* she had asked in the early morning, her face hanging over Ivy's. *When will you?* They had to stop the wireless because she got too excited by the news of the war. She was not upset by it; she must not have understood, Bear said. They have had to pretend that the wireless is broken.

We go to heaven, darling, Ivy said to Artemis now. She thought of how she had felt, under the water after the funeral: how would she describe this to her daughter, were she to try? Bear had told her, in the weeks afterwards, of the way she murmured about peace for the first few seconds after she could breathe again, before she slid into unconsciousness, limp in his arms. Ivy went to church each Sunday, but often she thought it was simply because it was the only time she was ever alone, Baby pulling on her skirts as she left, the Sunday air expectant. Ivy still hated sermons: when Reverend Giles spoke for any length of time she let her mind become clear as a flat ocean. She launched herself on its plains: she concentrated on her breath, as she had seen Angus do, years ago, his eyes closed, his legs crossed before him.

Bear put on his hat and jacket: he leant down and kissed the girls in turn, Baby flinching slightly as he did so. Then he kissed Ivy, not simply a peck but a long press of contact, his hands on her waist. She felt her body responding: it was a mechanism, a clock that Bear knew how to operate. It helped the days go more smoothly. Ivy thought of their small, wartime wedding – autumn sunlight filtered through stained glass, a simple white dress made by Anne, sandwiches in triangles on their best plates. And Artemis: already turning inside her, nudging Ivy's ribs as she said her vows. There was the sense that everything would be peaceful, from now on, if not in the world – or even in their own family, with Marina's lingering disapproval – then at least between them, within their affections. But the heart was so delicate, it seemed, so much less robust than that loyal lion of the body, still rising to Bear's touch.

Will you have a visitor today? He worried about her, being out here alone. She nodded. *Of course, darling.* She smiled.

At first, left alone with the children, she thought it was the closing of the door that did it, the particular noise it sent through the house, the way the whole structure had to re-adjust afterwards, the cracks widening, she imagined, the draughts getting worse. It was a noise like a bell tolling, signifying the shift from one mode of life to the next, from family – with its pockets of expectation, its tired, stable tropes – to a woman with her children beside her. A woman with her offspring was not a category that Ivy felt had been shaped for her: she did not know how to inhabit it. At home, as a child, there had always been Angus, or Gilbert, and then Anne, as well as Marina. She had never experi-enced this tense, weighted trio, both girls looking to her, at every moment, for the meaning of things.

She took a series of long, flat breaths, pictured the ocean before her – it was never a river – the endlessness of its vistas, the contrast to the small views she had here, from one room to the next. She put the porridge pan into the sink, thought of the description of Brother Lawrence she had read just yesterday: *even often while he is still busy, his very soul, without any forethought on his part, is lifted above all earthly things, main-tained and as it were upheld in God.* She breathed, moved the cloth around the pan. Behind her, Baby banged a spoon on her highchair as Artemis leant forward, wanting. *Can I have some more porridge, Mummy?* Artemis's voice was desperate, as though this was the tenth time she had asked, instead of the first.

It's all gone, darling. Shall I make you some toast?

She took the bread out, found a knife. *Above all earthly things.* She had often thought, illogically, that the question of her life would be solved by a single moment of unity: to be with her children, with their tender, blotched skin, and yet somehow to transcend, to lift herself to the peace she glimpsed so occasionally. Reverend Giles had told her that motherhood is the greatest vocation a woman can have. *After all*, he'd said, *look at Mary.* Ivy had read the annunciation over and over in her old school Bible, tearing the thin page slightly at its base. *The Holy Spirit will come upon you* – is that what happened to her, she wondered, on the Easter Joseph died?

She had read of sightings going back hundreds of years, an Abbot in Colchester, 1362, the craft he saw emerging, the great ship in the air of a blue dawn, a young moon surrounded by shining stars. She could imagine it, the shape like a balloon, birds flying from trees, afraid. When she told Gilbert about the light he had seemed interested, at first: if there could be an answer, perhaps Joseph could be saved, he seemed to think, even in death. He had murmured, for days, about *military operations*, about *secret projects*. By the funeral he had dismissed it. But then, months later, it was mentioned in the investigation into Joseph's death – there was a military base nearby, it was noted. *Reports of unusual lights in the sky.* But the investigation had given no further details, and now he refused to discuss it. It must have been a farmer out lamping, he said, though that never happened on Easter Sunday. A flame, then. An oil lantern blown and somehow alight on the breeze.

But Ivy wondered, still – she had read of the star of Bethlehem, of the shepherds, the glory of God shining around them. Of Moses and the burning bush. Angels descending to earth. Extraordinary things have happened, on extraordinary days. But what of all the other days? she wondered. It was time that was the difficulty: plain, ordinary time with its toast forks and milk upset on the floor – Baby had just flung hers, in a great, dismissive gesture – this was when she needed transcendence the most, and yet it evaded her. What sort of God would choose to be absent? She wanted to ask Reverend Giles this question, again. She wanted, in fact, to run to a headland – they were miles from the real sea – and shout it into the horizon. But she knew she would not.

Artemis was getting down from her chair now: she seemed to have forgotten about the toast. Ivy thought of calling her back, opened her mouth and closed it again. She knelt on the ground with a piece of old towelling, sopping up milk, watching the way it filled the material and dripped out again, its progress against the floor tiles. Was God here? she wondered, feeling foolish. Was He in this stinking rag?

She eased herself up from the ground; she was twenty-five and not sure if this was how her body should feel, used and hollow, as though her youth had been taken out, invisibly, replaced by air, or something liquid and useless, salt water perhaps, a sour sloshing.

She lifted Baby from her chair, felt the snapped clasping of the child's legs around her own body. She could believe, sometimes, that divinity was here, in the ease of her daughters' love for her, their beauty shining through dailyness, like a lick of fire over newspaper. Last week, she had lain in the cramped tin bath with Artemis, felt them both floating upwards, held in a light of love so pure and easeful she could believe it was holy. After church, she sometimes imagined it: the marked, bearded figure of Jesus, making His way barefoot up the lane. She would give Him tea, she thought. The girls would sit on His knees.

In the sitting room, Artemis was drawing with crayons, lines of scribble, impersonations of writing. *You should teach her to read*, Genevieve always said when she came. *I was reading at three.* Genevieve was interested in Artemis, considered her extraordinarily intelligent, as she herself had been at that age. Genevieve was one of the visitors that Bear arranged for her, dropped off by Hector at the top of the lane, teetering her way to the front door, a fur coat on, even in spring. She always brought books, as though she expected to read. On other days, there was Marina, with a pork pie baked by Anne wrapped in brown paper. Flowers from her garden. Marina sat in a chair in the kitchen and smoked: she talked about the galleries that were taking Angus's pictures, and not her own, of a recent notice written on Angus's work that described him as *a genius*. Angus had continued to go out when he was in London, drinking in the bars that were still open, even going to the theatre, despite Marina's protests. *Entirely unnecessary*, she would say, talk of the city somehow out of place at Ivy's small kitchen table.

When Artemis or Baby passed her by she ruffled their hair, touched their shoulders, or cheeks, or earlobes. Ivy remembered how, when she was a child, Marina liked to touch Ivy all the time. Touch her without seeing her, it sometimes felt, her nails across Ivy's scalp, down her back. She would lean over, absent-minded, and kiss her shoulder, her cheek, her thumb. She would carry on talking. Watching Marina with her grandchildren produced the memory of a sensation, a closeness, as strong as their separation was now. She wondered if this was inevitable, if her daughters would feel the same way about her: this pulling on a leash, the way distance felt not like freedom but disorientation, indifference. Ivy sat down now with Baby, helped her to grip a crayon, to copy her sister in her scrawling. *Mine!* Baby cried, making a rip through the page. Ivy thought of her Bible: she sighed, fetched her more paper. *Calmly*, she said into the top of Baby's head. *Gently.*

So much of motherhood was formed by this state of observation, of intervention: she was like the umpire at a tennis game, Ivy sometimes felt, but down on the ground rather than perched, imperious, over the scene. She looked at the door, so recently closed. She thought of the moment Bear would enter again, restore them to normality. There was no guessing his mood: when it was sombre – the war effort is failing, Germany is gaining ground – Ivy and the girls limped on to bedtime, their hope faltering, found only in sleep.

A few months ago Bear returned in a state of great excitement, his cheeks flushed, his coat still on as he spoke. *You'll never guess who I saw on the train?*

Ivy hated games like these: they tired her. *Angus?* Angus went to London even more often recently: he had a lover, it was said, a young artist with a shock of black hair who spoke wildly, made controversial statements about everything. Marina hated him, of course, much as she had once hated Bear, when he too had loved Angus. Even after Bear pulled Ivy from the river Marina could still, for a time, slip into sourness, even hatred, her eyes narrowing when Ivy mentioned Bear once too many. She had barely accepted the marriage, and never welcomed it, had behaved badly at the wedding. But when Artemis was born the softening had begun: as a baby she looked so like Bear, with her almost circular blue eyes, her tufts of blonde hair rising vertically from her scalp. Even Marina, in her mild resistance to grand-motherhood, could not ignore the physical reality of this child, who from a young age would hold up her arms to be cuddled and shout for *Ganny*. So, gently, almost impercept- ibly, Bear and Marina had begun to be friends. *He has such good taste*, she always says of him now. *Such a gentleman.* The children had placated her, in this regard at least, their smoothness like milk, coating any remaining bitterness.

And yet something else had shifted between Bear and Ivy, seemingly along with this, as though life were a stack of cards, a trick that could not be maintained. The children, beyond those greenhouse-close early days, had not enhanced their marriage, it seemed, but taken something from them, progressively, until love itself felt finite, endangered.

No, not Angus, Bear said now, impatiently, feeling that she was not quite playing along. *Nobody like that.*

Ivy was silent: she waited for him to tell her.

Frances! Do you remember her? Joseph's – girl. A slight pause here, as there was after any mention of Joseph, as though the dead could not be included in the conversation of the living. Ivy had not spoken at all for a few minutes: there was a kind of irritation at first, at how the past could creep into the present, with no warning at all. And then, yes – excitement, as though the Frances of today would carry some wisp of the atmosphere of the past, the hopes of the time before that Easter. Now, when Ivy thought of that day, it was in sepia, in an orange gauze, every movement softened by the on- goingness of life. This was before death, she felt, before any fact of death in her life. It was, in some way, eternal. She had heard from Frances only once, in all these years, a brief card when the investigation into Joseph's death – a *ghastly business*, as Angus had put it – had been completed. *Inconclusive*, was the final verdict, and Ivy wondered why the inquest had been conducted at all, when they could all have said the same thing.

Such a coincidence! Bear had gone on to say, when Ivy said nothing, though it turned out to be no coincidence at all; Frances had chosen the area, she said, from all the rural parts of England accessible to London, that green skirt around the city. Her family lived in Scotland, but her husband, David, was in the reserved occupations just as Bear was, with a limp from childhood polio – and she had chosen this place that she could remember, where she had some faint sense of belonging. She had said this to Bear and Ivy when, six days later, they came to supper, she and David on one side of the table, two church candles dripping their wax on to saucers. They had brought their small daughter, Rose, who slept on the sofa in the next room, her thumb tucked into her mouth, one finger folded over her nose.

Afterwards, Ivy and Frances had smoked outside – it was a cold night, still barely spring. Ivy felt, as she so often did here, that she was breathing the night of the funeral, of that Easter, the same air, the same wind. How often had she wished to live in Paris, or New York, or even Blackpool – anywhere that did not share the smells of this place, its geography, the rush of its river. The two women spoke politely to each other at first, carefully: Frances was paler now, scrubbed back, her face free of make-up, free too from the soaring presence of early youth. Ivy recognized the bewildered, unfocused look in her eyes, the disarray of childbirth still present, that moment of opening, as though a hole had been made in the fabric of existence, slow to close, if it ever closed at all. And even before this: there had been Joseph, the world opened in another way.

I was not the same – after, Frances said. *Even when I went back to university. I couldn't focus. There was something holding me to that moment, to Joseph. Some – tightness. It has been a relief, to come back here. To give in to it, I suppose. After – running away.*

Ivy had nodded, taken a drag of her cigarette. *I understand,* she'd said. *That makes perfect sense.* It did. From that precise moment, they had been friends, something smooth and unspoken in it, no need for the usual months of gradual escalation, tea to dinner to confidences over wine. Ivy had heard, from Bear, of how Frances had been unable to finish her degree, had married David – a friend of her brother's – instead. They were united, it seemed, in this journey: from loss to war to motherhood over the space of just a few years, violent in their rapidity.

And now, here, today, Frances was coming: into this grey morning, ostensibly so that Rose and Artemis could play together – with Baby trailing along – but truly so that Ivy could see Frances. Frances was unlike all the other company Bear arranged, the suppliers of pies and flowers and advice. She relished honesty about the tedium of wifehood, of child-rearing: they delighted in it together, encouraging each other to new heights of dismissiveness before returning, abashed, to reality, to statements of love for their husbands and daughters.

Of course we love them, they said together. *Of course.*

By the time the door-knock came, amidst dusty chimes of ten o'clock from the mantelpiece, Ivy felt that she couldn't stay in the house. She saw that it couldn't hold her and the girls, was too small, that any house would be too small for their gigantic minds, the endless spread of their thoughts. She had read Brother Lawrence again, crouched in the privy with the door open while the girls swirled around the wooden shed, banging sticks and chanting. *Take care that you begin your actions, continue them, and finish them with an inward lifting of the heart to God.* All morning, she had attempted to lift her heart to God, as she tried to wipe Baby's bottom before her daughter ran away, laughing, as she prepared food that went uneaten, drinks that were spilt so soon after pouring. And how high had her heart reached? Ivy wondered. To the top of the roof of the outhouse? To the heights of the birds?

Frances and Rose are here! Ivy could feel that her voice was too high, forced-sounding; the girls looked at her, frowning, mistrustful. But when they opened the door – all three of their hands on its frame – Frances and Rose were there, just as she'd said, and the girls' faith – in their mother, in reality itself – was restored. Frances looked windswept, pink in her cheeks, a patterned scarf around her head. *We walked all the way, didn't we?* she said, turning to Rose. *But somebody wanted to be carried.* On her hip Rose was plump and sulking, her purpling lower lip turned out. Ivy opened her arms, and to her surprise Rose came to her, pressed her cold cheeks into her neck, her legs around her waist. *Oh! How lovely*, she said. And it was: the foreignness of someone else's child, their different texture and weight in her arms. It felt somehow intimate, to be holding Frances's daughter like this: she could smell their home, the layering of life that made their particular atmosphere, so different from hers. And there was something like approval, or even blessing, in the way the little girl wrapped herself so tightly around Ivy's body, accepted it around her own. Ivy sat down on a chair and waited until Rose opened in her arms, went to join Artemis and Baby, who were playing with a pull-along duck, the paint on its green beak peeling away.

Frances and Ivy retreated from the room so gently the girls didn't even look up. Artemis and Rose had taken charge of the duck, had handed Baby a lesser toy that she accepted, a single, teetering wooden soldier, its red helmet chipped. As she backed away Ivy saw the soldier clutched in her daughter's raw fingers, entirely at the small girl's mercy.

In the back yard, Frances passed Ivy a cigarette. Ivy felt self-conscious, of the messy yard, the girls' sticks left at odd angles, the door of the privy banging in the wind. It seemed ridiculous, that the house was apportioned this tiny outside space, when just beyond it were acres of open fields and downs, wide spaces rolling to the river. Humans liked to be closed in, it seemed, to live with bordered horizons, everything separate and clear.

How are you? Frances asked her, and Ivy knew she expected an honest answer. But she could not say that she had spent the morning trying – and failing – to divinize her earthly life. She could just imagine the way Frances's face would crumple into laughter, or pity; she was a rationalist, just as Joseph had been, her atheism a rebellious contrast to her vicar father, the pious mother who held teas in the vicarage garden. Once, at Oxford, she and Joseph had helped to hand out pamphlets aimed at separating chapels from colleges, removing the chaplains from their posts. Ivy had tried to talk about faith with Frances before, had stumbled, unprepared, into this rare gulf between them.

Fine, Ivy said, before laughing. *No – not fine. The girls have been difficult. Bear is on some big project – I'm not sure if he'll even be back tonight.*

Frances nodded, blew out her smoke. *David too. Must be something up – but when is there ever not?* Her hair was escaping her headscarf: Ivy had always presumed Frances was a brunette, underneath the blonde dye of her youth, but the hair that emerged was a dark red, she saw now, the colour of rusted copper, or the peeled trunk of a birch tree. She almost reached up and touched it: it seemed so out of place in the grey yard, the overcast sky. From inside the house came a curdled yell.

Baby, Ivy said, feeling a sudden rush of pity for her smaller child, always drooling, red-faced, left out. The mothers took their places in the sitting room again, on the hard armchairs that had come with the house, lowering themselves to the floor when the girls began to bicker or scream. When they had first moved in, Marina could not stop herself commenting on the ugliness of the house, its furniture, the lack of pictures on the walls. She had given Ivy one of her own, a close-up of a mantelpiece that you could hardly identify as Cressingdon. Ivy liked the colours, the strong pastels that almost merged together, so that one part of the scene became blurred with the next. But she did not look at the painting much; she had learnt to see through it, it seemed, to pretend it wasn't there.

They gave their daughters lunch, not eating properly themselves but leaning on the cooker as the girls ate, swiping a leftover crust of corned beef sandwich from their plates. Then the girls finished, running away to their toys, and Ivy and Frances ate everything they had left, almost a full meal in itself.

Shall we go for a walk? Frances gestured outside, to the lowering sky, the scent of the day, the promise of freshness, of future rain, that came through an open window. Frances must have felt it too, Ivy thought: the way the walls of the house pressed at them. Ivy poured a kettle of hot water into the sink and slid the dishes in. They would all put their rain-coats on; they would embrace the elements. *Yes, let's. We can always go to the forest,* said Ivy. *We can make dens.* She still found it strange, to say motherly things like this. She imagined them all, crouched in small places that smelt of leaves, the girls whispering and giggling, small hands held to their lips. She smiled at Frances, pushed her own hair from her eyes. Outside: a low, distant rumble of thunder came towards them across the hills.

It took them half an hour to wrestle the girls into their gumboots and mackintoshes, Artemis complaining that her new coat's arms were too long, Baby kicking off her stiff boots by accident, screaming until they were forced back on. But then they were out, freed not just from the house, Ivy felt, but the whole confinement of their lives, every hour accounted for, every moment predictable and yet chaotic, tuned to the whims of beings who did not yet know how to behave or think, who terrorized the world. Surely, Ivy thought, her own childhood had been nothing like this: she remembered days trailing around the garden alone, her skin caked as though by an oven, a rough second skin of mud formed across her knees. She was always dirty, unobserved, collecting fruit for Anne or buttercups for Marina. She remembers moving through the grass, picking up small plums which bruised and swelled under her fingers, thinking of Anne's face, when she delivered the fruit to her, how pleased she would be. Ivy had once thought she might be a cook before Marina told her it was *most unsuitable*, for a girl like her.

A soft rain began to fall as they left; rain in wartime felt somehow appropriate, more so than the beautiful, flawless days which planes sliced through, and occasionally dropped out of, as though from nowhere. Just last month a German plane had crashed in a nearby field, the smoke visible from the cottage. There were stories of two German soldiers still strapped to their seats, of villagers standing back, nobody running to save them.

Now, they walked through the damp landscape, the older girls running ahead and back to them, Baby holding Ivy's hand, her plump fingers slipping, regrasping. The rain had made the scents of flowers rise, giving the day a humid, almost sultry feeling, the fertility of the soil mineral, tangible in the air.

Remember how Joseph loved storms?

Frances turned to her: she was smiling. When they spoke about Joseph, it often seemed that he had loved everything. Christmas, and baked ham, and cakes with raisins. Particular composers and then all composers – as though his life were one long uninterrupted moment of joy. He *was* lucky, Ivy thought now. So often laughing, open. And in love.

For a long time, Ivy had expected Joseph to walk into a room where she sat. To hear his laugh across the fields. She had heard that there could be lasting effects, from a near-drowning, some part of the brain for ever sodden and ill-tuned. Perhaps she was delusional. Then one day she real-ized she'd been hoping for a resurrection – it had been Easter, after all – for Joseph's death to have been some ter-rible cosmic mistake, a reversible slip in the order of things. She remembered her childish enthusiasm for the story of Easter, the image of Mary Magdalene running back from the tomb, breathless. This felt real, to Ivy: that a woman should be the first to know, and that she should run like that. Ivy had denied, for years, her hope that she would see Joseph again. And in fact she *had* seen him – in the turn of a man's head in the Underground or the bank, even now, occasion-ally, in the blanched face of a boy back from war, or the gentle hands of the postman, a certain way he bent down to a dog. But she always shook herself, looked away and back again to an unfamiliar face, or the hands of a stranger, telling herself Joseph was gone.

Ivy realized what would happen before she had time to pre-vent it: she saw the familiar bend of the trees, the pattern of trunks instantly recognizable. Cressingdon, the woods at its edge, the river audible now, rushing just feet away. She had become used to skirting this area with the girls on most of their walks, but they had begun to recognize trees, to see the world around them so much more clearly. Frances, she knew, had not been back since the funeral. She was always meaning to, she said, but Ivy sensed she was afraid.

Can we see Granny? Artemis asked, running back with Rose, both of them grinning, kicking up mud with their boots, Rose's dark red hair tucked into the back of her mackintosh.

And Annie! And Angus?

Ivy paused. She was stupid, she saw now, not to have considered this. She wanted to keep walking with Frances, for them to breathe the same air, see the same things. At Cressingdon, she would be with the adults, in the realm of paintings, talk of London and lovers. Marina's moods were unpredictable: grandchildren aside, she had not softened with age, as people had said she would. How would she respond, Ivy wondered, to seeing Frances?

But Artemis had made her eyes wide in the way that preceded a tantrum. She had sensed her mother's hesitation and was ready to resist, to turn her will into the world-altering force it could be. *Don't give in to her,* Ivy was always saying to Bear. *Don't give her what she wants.* But he couldn't stand to listen to her crying: he simply wanted it to stop. Artemis had learnt to turn her face to a single red-purple blotch, spreading, widening from her features to all that surrounded her. Even Rose took a step back, held on to her mother, her fingers whitening.

I'm not sure we have time? Ivy looked at Frances, smiling gently, allowing her the chance to pull back, even now, to visit another day. But Frances only returned her smile. *I'm sure we can go for a little while. We can warm up a bit, can't we?*

She was speaking to Rose, as though to convince her, squeezing her hand.

Hooray! Artemis jumped on the spot; Ivy felt a wave of resentment turn over within her, as though her daughter were fourteen instead of four. She knew how grown-up her elder child could appear to her, if only by comparison with her younger. She had expected so much of her, from the moment Baby was born, Artemis's head and hands enormous, clumsy, as she clambered over the bed. She was happy now; singing to herself, picking tiny flowers from the ground. There was something about her grandparents' house that was a relief to Artemis, Ivy sensed, a letting-go of some burden found in her own home.

They picked their way slowly through the woodland, Baby falling and crying but refusing to be carried, her hands becoming stained with dirt. *It looks just the same*, Frances was saying. *It's always the same*, Ivy replied. *Although there are new paintings now – they've been busy.* She raised her eyebrows, as though speaking about amateurs rather than world-renowned artists, late middle-aged now, rising into their time of reputation, of easy acceptance to galleries. There were even solo shows on the horizon, Marina had told Ivy at her last visit. *But I don't care about that*, she'd said, waving a hand through her own smoke.

They approached Cressingdon over the back lawn, the house rising into view, the glass of the studio clouded by reflections, the doors to the garden room closed. Anne appeared at the kitchen window, her head floating, pale. *Annie!* Artemis ran towards her, expectant of Anne's warm, soft body, of the cake she was no doubt keeping in a tin. Even with rations, Anne managed to carry on baking most days, to fill the house with that particular rising sweetness. It was sorcery, Marina said, though Anne kept chickens in a corner of the garden, and Ivy knew Angus bought whatever Marina wanted on the black market. Even Bear had backhanders sometimes, delicacies that he would take to Cressingdon, present like offerings on a shrine.

Anne's eyes filled when she saw Frances, and Ivy saw that Frances too, was moved, overwhelmed, even, by the sight of Anne, of the house, the garden, so present and unchanging.

How lovely to see you again, dear. Anne was gazing at Frances, seeing Joseph in her, Ivy imagined, seeing the days themselves playing across her face.

Why are you all looking at each other? Artemis's voice, as though breaking a spell. They laughed, returned to themselves, to the present.

Inside, Ivy and Frances bustled around the girls, removing coats and boots, fetching glasses of water. They all sat around the kitchen table, Anne leaning her hands across it, holding Ivy's fingers, warming them in her own.

Are you eating enough? she asked. *You look so thin.*

Ivy looked at Frances.

I get plenty of leftovers, Ivy said, smiling. The kitchen door opened, and Marina was there, in her smock streaked with paint, light blues and greys across her hands, the colour of a spring sea. For a moment Ivy thought the whole visit had been a mistake. Marina looked disorientated, her hair uncovered, striking out at strange angles. Perhaps if the children hadn't been with them, she would have looked curiously at Ivy, asked why she was there, as though she barely recognized her. She had done that before. But she loved the children. She pounced on the girls, one after the other, Baby raising her hands above her head to touch her grandmother's face. *Darlings! And who is this pretty one?* She stopped in front of Rose.

This is Rose, Frances said. *My daughter.*

It was only now that Marina seemed to see Frances. She raised one hand to her mouth; Ivy felt herself holding her breath.

Marina's eyes widened. *Daughter? Of course.*

She nodded two, three times, as though returning to reality, reminding herself that this was not Joseph's daughter. That this child – with her wisping hair, her close, dark eyes – was nothing to do with Joseph.

Well, very pleased to meet you, Rose. And lovely to see you, Frances. Just lovely. I'm sure Anne has given you – yes, I see, cake already! Wonderful. She moved back to the doorway. *Frances, Ivy, would you like to come through?*

Frances hesitated, and Ivy looked to Anne.

Oh, I'd love to watch these little ones, Anne said. *We'll have fun, won't we, ladies?*

The older girls cheered. Marina did this, on some visits: separated the children from the adults, left them to knead dough with Anne in the kitchen, their chaos contained to a single room. For all her sparks of grandmotherly joy, Ivy knew Marina considered herself finished with children, beyond the point at which they could interfere with the free movement of her life. If she wanted to speak with Ivy and Frances alone, she would do so.

Marina led them into the studio, through the hallway where Ivy and Bear had kissed for the first time all those years ago, the floorboards shining as they always had. Ivy noticed the way that memory functioned differently now, fell upon her lightly, as though she had raised a shield against it. She only felt the memory of a memory – an image of Bear's lips on hers, but not the original sensation, not the particular moment of its happening: the sun that day, the smell of his clothes.

In the studio, the light was dim from the darkness of the day outside; there were lamps everywhere, like a bazaar, making the colours of the paintings even warmer, the fabrics that were draped across the furniture, the intricate rugs on the floor. In one corner, a painting was in the midst of creation, the brush still wet and resting on an easel. *The brush is everything*, Marina once said to Ivy. *It is my whole life.* Seeing a painting like this always felt forbidden, to Ivy: like glimpsing a man's stomach under his shirt when he lifted his arms.

She looked away, but Frances moved closer, began to study the canvas from every angle.

Marina took a seat at the coffee table; she motioned for Ivy and Frances to do the same.

What are you doing now, Frances? she asked, shaking a cigarette from its pack. Her fingers were trembling very slightly, Ivy noticed. *I always remember you writing for the student paper, wasn't it? Joseph used to – show us your articles. Terribly good, weren't they, Ivy?*

Ivy nodded, though felt within her a slow collapse of shame; she had never bothered to read Frances's articles, when she was younger. She remembered Joseph placing one next to her breakfast, where she spilt egg yolk across it. Joseph had been angry; now, she wonders if Marina remembers this, if that was why, in some strange way, she had mentioned it.

Well. Frances smoothed down her skirt, looked up again, smiling. *I don't write any more – I'm so busy, with the house and—*

Just Rose, is it? Marina was tapping her cigarette into a misshapen tortoise on the table, its belly caved in to make a well for the ash. Joseph had made it, Ivy remembered. At school. She also remembered how proud he was when he brought it home, cradled in his damp palm.

Yes, just Rose. Frances let out her breath, the impersonation of a laugh. *But she keeps me busy enough.*

Really? You couldn't fit a little piece in around nap time, perhaps? Don't we know someone at The Times, *Ivy? We could ask—*

Oh, leave her alone, Mother. Ivy tried to say this in a jocular way, light at the ends, but she could see Marina beginning to retract herself, preparing for fury. Ivy rushed on:

Mother always asks me if I'm painting. And I say yes! Painting that chipped front door!

Her voice sounded strange, she knew, but Frances looked at her gratefully. There was a noise from outside: a kind of yelling, a youthful bustle too large to be their children. Ivy saw Marina's face shift entirely, a soft woundedness around her lips. But then she recovered. *Oh! That must be Angus and – and – Charles.* A too-full smile now, on this name.

So they would meet Charles, Angus's latest favourite, and *something serious* this time, according to Bear. He was *practically living* at Cressingdon, Bear had said. *Marina's furious – but saying nothing, of course.*

And now they were here, like two boys, bounding in from the garden, Charles raising his hand, almost bashfully.

Hullo—

Ivy felt something in her chest rearrange itself: this was just the way Joseph used to come into the studio, like a bull, Marina always said. And wasn't there something in his energy that matched that of the paintings themselves, something entirely appropriate? Ivy thought of this now as she watched Charles, with his long black hair that he flicked away in great gestures of his large, flat hands. Wasn't he around the age Joseph would have been, now? His mid-twenties, rising into his physical prime, still with that shade of uncertainty.

Angus was obviously surprised; he was probably expecting the studio to be empty, with the sounds of children in the kitchen. But when he turned to them his face was open with charm: he knew how to be friendly, to open at least the top layer of himself, to present it to the world.

Frances? He swallowed, nodding slowly. *You've hardly changed.* This was manifestly untrue; Frances's face was drawn, her hair and figure transformed by childbearing, by years of rationing. Marina and Angus were insulated from the war, Gilbert was always saying so; they had created an island of peace, their own country of art and gentle music, of dinner at eight. Gilbert lived in London now, worked at the Ministry of Information, was often not back at home until ten or eleven, and then spent the night in shelters. *Marina and Angus live in a fantasy*, he had said to Ivy. *A play of their own creation.* She could see Gilbert now, hunched tightly over his large desk, round glasses sliding down his nose. She often saw posters and wondered if he had written them. *Hints to Mothers*, a recent one had read. *Learn to put on baby's gas helmet quickly, while wearing your own mask.* How would Gilbert feel, writing this? Would he be as appalled as she was, reading it? Or had he become used to it? *Toddlers soon learn to put on their own masks*, the poster had continued. *Let them make a game of it, and they will wear their gas masks happily.* She thought of Baby's screams whenever they had tried – even for a few seconds – to drag a mask over her head.

Now, Angus pulled a chair out for himself and Charles,

leant in over the table, taking a cigarette from Marina's packet.

Are you interested in art? he asked Frances. *I could show you around a bit – if you'd like. We've got lots that's new here. Not just by us old goats.*

He chuckled in a way that was meant to be self-deprecating, took a long drag on his cigarette. He was renewed, Ivy could see, by Charles, though the young man's youth also seemed to shade Angus's own age, to force him to mention it.

Oh, yes, that would be wonderful. A lightness came over Frances's face. *I never see art these days.*

I'd love an update too, Ivy said. *Has Charles had a tour yet?*

I haven't— Charles looked at her. And then at Angus—

Well, not exactly— A smile, unquestionably flirtatious.

Ivy did not look, but knew Marina was staring. Ivy did not often goad her mother: she had grown out of the habit when she saw what could follow, the soaring rages, Marina seeming to grow ten feet tall before collapsing, becoming meek again, nursed by Anne. But Ivy liked Charles, instantly, liked the new dimension he brought to the room, the way his presence felt – even smelt – like life itself, like London and wine, small studios filled with smoke.

Angus walked them into the large drawing room, almost every inch of wall covered by art. Painting was their religion, Ivy saw now, more clearly than ever before: they directed everything towards it. This was Marina's chapel, Angus her priest. Ivy would tell Gilbert this, when they spoke again: it was not a play, after all, but a monastery, a space carved from the world. *Silly Rabs*, she could imagine Gilbert saying. *What notions you have.*

After a few minutes, Ivy found herself tuning out Angus – his name-dropping, his casual descriptions of whole movements in art – but Frances looked captivated, touching his arm, laughing loudly when he said something amusing. Angus was still handsome, his mouth curled and suggestive, his hair thick and full. He had come alive for Frances, his skin pinking, his voice loud, as though speaking to a great crowd. Charles watched the two of them, his eyebrows raised as though amused. Marina had stayed in the studio.

Of course, Charles himself is an outstanding painter—

Ivy let the others move on; she had found herself in front of a painting in a black frame. It was over the piano, so she had to lean forward to see it, adjust her eyes in the dim light. It was an abstract work, by a painter she didn't recognize. Most of the canvas was blue, with two pink shapes like gigantic people, the size of whales, partly in and out of the water. Something about it intrigued her: the depth of its darkness, the mystery it evoked. Reverend Giles had lent her a book about St John of the Cross; she had not understood most of it, but one phrase from his poetry had remained with her: *exquisite risk*. Where was this, she wondered, in this comfortable world of sofas and flowers in vases? Where was the risk? She supposed it was here: in the brushstrokes, the attempt to create life on the canvas. But she found – had always found – that she wanted more, for the risk to be discovered outside the studio. In life itself.

There was a sound like a horse running in the hallways, a rhythmical pounding that grew louder and louder until the door was open and the girls were there, ecstatic, bursting, their cheeks smeared with jam. *A storm's coming! A storm's coming!* Rose and Artemis chanted it like little witches, running in circles, Baby stomping behind, joining in as much as she could. Then Anne was at the doorway, breathless, apologetic.

Sorry – I couldn't – they're very excited. Ivy looked out of the window: hadn't a storm been coming all afternoon? But the sky was thickly black now, the clouds bulging from themselves, bubbling like treacle in a pan.

They all stood and stared: *Have you ever seen?* It looked so unusual Ivy could almost believe it was something to do with the war – they were doing experiments, didn't the news say? Complicated new weapons, chemical tests. But Angus said they were called *stratus clouds*. He had seen them before, he said, but only far out at sea, sailing with his father. *It'll be a storm, all right*, he said. He looked excited, his sleeves rolled up, a certain energy in his movements, as though he might be about to paint the sky. Charles too looked thrilled: Ivy could imagine him running through the rain with his arms open, yelling and cheering at the top of his voice. She had never met him before, and yet she felt she could predict his actions: perhaps, she realized, it was Joseph she was imagining, after all.

The lightning was a shock; a flat expanse of brightness, a bleaching exposure of the landscape. Then there was thunder, deep and rumbling, the turning over of the earth. Baby held on to Ivy's leg, and even Artemis moved closer, within touching distance. They all counted the seconds: five, or more. *Do we have time to run back, do you think?* Ivy looked to Frances: she thought of the alternative, of waiting out the storm at Cressingdon. With Angus. With Marina. Perhaps Frances sensed it. She laughed, bundled Rose into her arms. *I think we might* she said, tickling the little girl, both of them seeming to squeal with bravery. *Let's try.*

This time, they were dressed quickly, the girls excited, sensing the electricity in the air, the world becoming denser. They called out goodbyes, to Marina, and Angus, and Anne, who stood at the door waving in unison, as though they were setting out on a great voyage, instead of walking a mile down the road. From the children, there was no moaning, no tripping over. They made it to the woods swiftly, clambering over tree trunks and vines, the older girls helping the younger, Baby's boots landing with a thud on the soft ground. Ivy could feel her body working in a way it rarely did any more, her heart responding to the excitement, her legs still strong under her. She was not old. She had children, but her body was ready and willing. After the woodland was a stretch of open fields: above them the sky creaked with fullness, the light that grew around the clouds yellowing, hazed, so that everything coloured – the grasses of the fields, the girls' mackintoshes and boots, Frances's and Rose's hair – all appeared shining, unnaturally bright, as though lit up from within.

There was lightning, then more thunder, much closer this time, making the girls jump and yell and run faster. *We might not make it*, Frances said, her breath coming thick now, her face shining with effort. They were entering the last part of the route, all five of them elated. There was a single drop on Ivy's finger, another on her face, but there would be time, surely, plenty of time before the clouds let go entirely, before the land was covered in water. They were at the stile now, the house visible before them, its air of resigned indifference. *Nearly there!* Ivy yelled at the girls; there was another tumble of thunder and it happened: they were covered, suddenly, in another place, another world whose element was water. It was heavier than any rain Ivy had been in: it felt as though a bucket had been turned over in space. It was a *deluge*, she thought: this was the word.

If she had been alone with the girls, Ivy might have been afraid. She would have lifted them both and tried to run, slipping, calling out reassurances in a broken falsetto. But with Frances, she found that she could not be afraid: fear was not part of the world they created together, this small coven of women and girls. The trees were blown sideways and seemed to have turned blue, the whole sky riven, the grasses risen and wild, the soil deepening with every step. And yet they remained upright, just as the world did: they were intact.

Good grief! Frances shouted, as a particularly strong gust of rain blew against them, but she kept moving, the girls kept moving, Baby only looking back to check with her mother, to be assured of her safety. And then they were in the yard, and at the door, Ivy fumbling with keys, all of them breaking through and gasping, drenched, looking at one another.

They crouched beside their daughters first, stripping off their sodden clothes – the rain had passed straight through their coats – and laying them on a rack beside the fireplace.

I'll make a fire, said Ivy, but she herself was soaked, her skin cold and clammy, her sleeves dripping on to the carpet.

I'll lend you some clothes, she said to Frances, and turned to go upstairs, leaving the girls in their dry underthings, playing again with the duck and soldier on the small circle of carpet. Though she had not asked her to, Frances followed, her steps a few feet behind Ivy's. It felt strange, to have Frances in their bedroom, the large bed somehow embarrassing, with its mismatched pillowcases, its blankets that the girls had whipped into a tangle. Ivy thought, for a moment, of the bedroom they had stood together in, the night Joseph died, of the way even the furniture seemed alive, then, and to be watching them. From downstairs, as though from the future, there came a sharp yell, a cry of *Mummy!* She began to rummage in drawers, in the wardrobe; when she turned around Frances was undressing, as though it was nothing, as though they were girls at school.

There was no time to look away: she saw the looseness of Frances's stomach above her girdle, so like Ivy's own, the fossilized white patterning of stretch marks leading up to her brassiere, the same simple type of garment Ivy wore now, her chest emptied and filled, re-formed by breastfeeding. The skin of Frances's body was a warmer tone than she had expected, reddish like her hair, and seeming to radiate softness. Ivy gave her a blouse, looking at the carpet – *hopefully this will fit you*, she said. She went downstairs.

If Bear was not home by dark he would not be at all. This was the rule they had agreed between them, no telephone in the house and not a phone box for miles. Bear had tried to get one fitted but there were not the wires for it, apparently, they did not stretch to sloping old cottages in the middle of nowhere. Outside, the sky still held traces of daylight, pink and purple, as though bruised by the storm. Ivy knew Cressingdon would still be visible, from the upper windows, Anne beginning to hang the blackout. In the cottage, the air had become moist with drying clothes, something almost tropical about the scent of soap mixed with the tired exertion of their daughters, their play relentless, building in its expectations, roles, the scripts subtly changing with each new round. Frances and Ivy had managed an entire pot of tea without interruption, Frances sitting on a kitchen chair with legs tucked under her, her hair wisping out from behind her ears, thumb curled around the base of her teacup. Every few minutes, Ivy had found herself startling at a different noise – the cows in the next field, the bang of a farmer's van – thinking it was Bear. She could feel it, along her skin, the way the house changed in his presence, as though every element gathered itself, stood to attention. He made it real, she often thought, but there was something rigid, in this reality, something that refused to yield to the loose, watery streams of sensation. In this way, Ivy thought without wanting to, he was like her mother.

No sign of Bear, she said to Frances now, unable to prevent herself from letting him enter their conversation, which prior to this had meandered gently around their daughters, and back to themselves, like tracing a path across your palm, the stories barely visible, almost secret, intersecting at unknown points.

From next door came a cry: the play had, at last, broken down, descended into tears and accusations. Ivy and Frances exchanged the briefest of looks before returning to the girls, to the crier, who was Baby of course, wet and hot with tears, scooped in Ivy's arms, promised a biscuit.

Frances glanced at the window, where darkness had fallen, entire, totalizing in the blackout.

Silly of me, she said, beginning to rush, to pack their things
into her wicker basket. Ivy hated to think of them stumbling
along on the lane. She hated, she realized, to think of them
leaving at all.

You could stay? She said it quickly. *We have the camp beds?
The girls would love it, I'm sure* . . . Frances stopped, her hand
on Rose's teddy bear, its one remaining eye hanging slightly
loose. *Well, David won't be back either, I suppose, if Bear isn't.*
She turned to Rose. *Shall we stay the night, darling? Shall we
have an overnight stay, with Artemis and Baby?* Rose held her
hands closed beneath her chin, like a picture in a children's
prayer book, her perfect white teeth in a row above them.

Yes, Mummy! Yes, please.

Well, that's decided then, said Frances, squeezing one of
Rose's cheeks. *We'll stay – have a little celebration. For surviving
the storm.* She turned to Ivy. *I don't suppose – you have anything
to drink?*

There was some gin that they were saving for Bear's birthday – Ivy did not pause before fetching it, telling herself it
could be replaced. There were pork chops in the cold box,
for the weekend, and she fetched these too, left them to
breathe on the sideboard. They would have meat, and potatoes; they would have drink. The two women cooked
together, wordlessly adding salt, a little more water, sipping
their gin, humming tunes. The kitchen became a place of
low mists, the texture of meat in the frying pan, the bubble
of potatoes under boiling water. Next door, the girls played

happily, buoyed into a state of harmony, playing at kindliness, giving Baby turns with the duck.

It amazed Ivy, how simple this all was with Frances, how domestic life had become a party, borderless and open. With Bear, they seemed held within an outline that neither of them had chosen, but could not renounce. They were mother, father, children: the home was hushed, procedural, or ancient-seeming, like a fairy tale, their days dense with association, with the layering of their own childhoods, their parents' childhoods before them. *No elbows on the table*, Bear would tell the girls, and Ivy would repeat what he said. *Listen to your father*, she said. *Do as he tells you*. But when she and Frances ate with the girls, nobody told anybody what to do. When the girls were silly, she and Frances laughed. They were silly themselves. It was a break, Ivy told herself, it was a holiday. Normal life could never be like this. But she held the moments, even as they were happening, tried to press them to herself, or to the walls around her, tried to make her life – this house – absorb some of their joy.

Filled with meat and potatoes, the girls' bodies were solid as Ivy undressed them, heavy arms and legs that she lifted and clothed before they fell back to the sheets, dense as stones. Frances helped her check the blackout, then perched on the end of Artemis's bed, Rose on the low camp bed below her. She read the girls *The Tale of the Flopsy Bunnies*, her voice rising and falling, never leaving the rich valley of its tone, the resonance that reminded Ivy of a woman she had once seen playing the cello, years ago, in a concert in London, her long hair falling over the instrument's turns, over the bow as she had moved it. Ivy had the strange sense, leaning on the door frame, that she would have liked Frances to be her mother, or her sister, as she would have been, she supposed, had she married Joseph. It was this she longed for – this particular voice as company, lowering her daughters into sleep.

Afterwards, they closed the door softly, Baby's snores already audible from her cot. They cleared the toys from the sitting room together, on their knees, throwing them into the wooden chest. *I have never liked toy boxes*, Marina had said on one visit. *Such confusion . . .* But Ivy closed the lid, and all the jumble disappeared beneath the smooth wooden surface. The sitting room was a room again, instead of a nursery: they could smoke there now; they could talk.

I'm sorry, Ivy said, *about my mother earlier. She's – intrusive.*

Frances looked down, brushed a thread off her lap.

Nobody ever asks me about my writing any more. I don't know what to say. Are you still . . . painting?

Definitely not. Ivy laughed. *I don't have any worldly ambitions any more.* The gin was bringing her close to honesty. Careful, she said to herself. Slow down.

Frances was smiling over her glass.

Because of the children?

No— Ivy said it before she could stop herself. *Not entirely.*

I just seem to have let go of all that, these days.

Frances nodded, blew out a cloud of smoke.

Well, Baby's so young. She's still – a baby.

Ivy sank her head into her hands.

We have to stop calling her that! It's her name now. Terrible of us.

Beyond the blackout there was a soft whirring, like an insect stuck between fabric and glass. Ivy had not felt close to the war all evening, even when they hung the curtains, the material thick and scratchy between her fingers. It had seemed ceremonial, even absurd, all part of the sense of festivity: and didn't the girls sleep better, anyway, without the morning sun coming through?

But here was another whirring: louder this time.

Buzz bombs, Frances said calmly. *We haven't had those for a while.*

There was a night, months ago, when Bear took Ivy to the roof and they had watched them, those strange silver shapes, floating towards London.

We could look – from the roof, she said to Frances, knowing they shouldn't. But *exquisite risk*, she thought: hadn't the best of the day been found in this?

As they climbed, they helped each other, much as the girls did in the forest that afternoon, Ivy leaning down from the flat roof of the kitchen to where Frances was balanced on a dustbin. Her hand felt strong, as it gripped; she thought she must be, to be able to pull a grown woman on to a building. Above them, the sky had cleared completely, as though all clouds – not only of that day, but of all days – had been pushed away. They could see every star, galaxies swirled like spilt cream above them. Ivy had brought a blanket; they leant against the slates that covered the bedroom wall: they pulled the wool around them. The sky was quiet: they could hear a rustle, a distant animal or bird.

No more bombs, said Frances. *After all that.* She rubbed her hands together for warmth.

We've become so used to it, haven't we? Do you ever think about – before?

Ivy nodded; she thought of Frances at the funeral, the way her face had dipped and opened, how she sat frozen beside Marina, swayed beside Genevieve.

Do you still have that coat? With all the animal buttons?

It's in the wardrobe, full of moth holes. David doesn't understand why I keep it—

—I don't think you should ever throw it away.

Ivy put her arm around Frances, an easy gesture, something friendly in it, protective. Frances rested her head against Ivy, her hair touching her nose, her chin against her breastbone.

Maybe I'll keep it for ever – give it to Rose, one day—

Frances lifted her head, to look at Ivy. But it was Ivy who leant forward first. Who kissed Frances, the imperfect contact of their lips somehow inevitable, perfect, making them reach for each other, for handfuls of fabric, for the warm reality of each other's skin. In those seconds Ivy felt the whole of Frances, present, rising; she knew she did not have to look for her beyond or behind the surface: Frances was there, in every touch, the experience not a mystery, now, but a confirmation. Ivy felt, for a moment, that she could be like Brother Lawrence, after all, God's presence in every movement she made. Perhaps, she thought – her fingers in Frances's hair – there was no separation between the world of objects and the world beyond. Maybe – her hand held the warm arc of Frances's neck – it had been one world, all along.

Years later, Ivy would remember this time on the roof as a single image, not the kiss itself, but the sight of Frances, in profile, her hair around her ears, her mouth opened to laugh. It was as though all of their love could be found there: it couldn't be true, she knew, and yet it was: every part of the world was entirely itself, and present for them. Frances had brought the last of the gin, and they shared it from one glass, its edge smooth on their lips.

The second time, the buzz bombs were seen before they were heard, some trick of light and sound, the long tube of silver in the distance, and then the noise: a swarm, a tempest of insects, coming towards them. They did not move, at first: hadn't this been their plan, to watch the bombs passing over them? But if it had seemed foolish before, now it seemed irrelevant, only distantly interesting, like the games of their younger selves. How strange they were, Ivy thought now, this invention, like squid in an endless ocean, forever seeking. Ivy followed one last bomb with her eyes, watching its progress over the land and fields, the woodland beside Cressingdon and beyond, over its garden. It was the engine of the bomb, Bear had told her, that made that sound; it pulsed fifty times a second. It was like a sped-up heart, he had said.

They were weapons that needed no people, that could find their own targets. There was a clearness, an absence of noise filled by the movement of trees, the call of a distant bird. The wind was increasing. Then Ivy realized: the engine had stopped. The noise had halted. The silver tube was tipping, dropping and falling, hundreds of miles from its destination. There was no time to speak, only a small, distant explosion, a puff of fire, so small from where they sat, like a spark from a sausage pan. Ivy heard Frances cry out. Before them, Cressingdon was lit, a torch in the blackout, a tear through the night.

Ivy looked at Frances; she was dumb, uncomprehending. *Go*, Frances said. *I'll stay with the children.* Ivy nodded – of course she should go – to help. To see them. To make sure— But she felt rooted, solid, infinitely heavy. Frances touched her arm; Ivy nodded again, blinking.

I'll be here, Frances said. *Don't worry. Go to Cressingdon.*

★

The lane was almost pitch-black – Ivy had brought a torch, but the beam kept flickering, uncertain of itself with every step. She walked by the road – it was a longer way, and as she walked she grew tired, seemed for some minutes to forget why she was walking, to enter a dream of nothingness, no fear, only the slap of her shoes against the rough stone of the path, the wind in her ears, flashes of light from the torch against the fields. But then there was a sound: the ringing – so close – of a fire engine's bell, that high, sinister rattle. And as she got closer, she began to smell it: fire, smoke, the sickening sweetness of burnt paper.

When she arrived it did not seem to be Cressingdon at all: this place of confusion – shouts, shadows, distant flames – could not be the place where she had grown up, the place of lunches on the lawn, cultured chatter dissolving into evening. This was a war place: officials in bright vests, figures in blankets, others with buckets, whistles, torches. The smell was almost unbearable now, the smell of her childhood turned against itself. It was the studio that was alight, Ivy could see now, its roof collapsing under streams of water that poured from the firemen's hoses. There were four of them – village volunteers perhaps – in their round hats, the metal studs of their jackets glowing in the remaining flames. Ivy tried to move forward, but was held back, an arm emerging from the darkness. Bear, she thought irrationally, but it was only the farmer from down the lane, face streaked with soot, his eyes made strange by fear.

The studio. The sweet smell of woodsmoke was now mixed with something less familiar: burning chemicals – *burning paint* – a complex sharpness in the air. Ivy began to shout, turning to release herself from the farmer's touch. *Mother! Angus! Anne!* She darted around the groups with her torch, every sight blurred into the next.

And there they were – Angus, Charles, Marina, Anne – in matching red blankets, sat on the lawn. They were facing away from the house, each a small distance from the other, Marina closer to Anne than Angus. Their faces were empty of expression, covered in grey soot, spectres of themselves. Behind them, the studio in charred ruins, smoke and small flames still rising from its wooden doors.

Ivy, Anne said, and held out her hands. *Darling,* Marina said, her voice fading into darkness.

Something shifted behind them; there was a sound of sizzling, of a small collapse somewhere within. How many paintings were in there? A hundred? Two hundred? Ivy thought of them all, on the walls, propped against furniture, stacked in their dozens in the storeroom. She could picture them intact, she found – whole, beautiful – but she could not picture them burning. It was unthinkable.

A painting will outlive a love affair, Marina had written this once, in one of her letters to Aunt Genevieve. But the paintings were gone. What did it mean, Ivy wondered, to create things that could be destroyed as easily as this? *We know God by His creatures*: she had read this in one of Reverend Giles's books; and yet here were the works of God's creatures: destruction, beauty turned to soot and ruin.

It would never be the same, Ivy realized at that moment. Whatever happened, the place she knew – had grown within – was gone for ever. She imagined Joseph's reaction: he would have run straight in there, she suspected. Tried to save what he could. She could see him, she imagined: a shadow at the edge of the flames. She looked back to the remains of her family, the survivors on the grass and the ruined building somehow the same, everything monotonized, greyed by ash. *Angus, Anne, Marina*: their names were a litany, their bodies like reflections in the broken studio glass, altered images, rising from the night.

The main house would need to be thoroughly checked and aired, the firemen said. Everyone would need to stay else-where, at least for tonight. Ivy's cottage was too small, of course – but Revd Giles had offered the spare bedrooms of his vicarage, and Marina had accepted, gratefully. Ivy helped her mother into an ambulance, feeling the lightness of her body against her shoulders. Marina's face was a wash of pale shock, her hands barely able to hold Ivy's for shaking. Behind her, Angus was bowed like a puppet as he dipped his head to climb in, his clothes streaked with soot and mess, his eyes blank. Charles came behind him, looking too young to face such a disaster, as out of place as he had once been at ease. Anne was the only one who seemed intact, upright, her solidity giving the sense, for a moment, that she was the mistress, and Angus and Charles and Marina her defeated servants.

As Ivy climbed out of the ambulance, the warden asked if she would be coming with them, his hands on the doors. Ivy paused. She thought of the moment she had left Frances at the door of the cottage, its seconds somehow evaporated into the staging of the night, the crisp air, its quickening pulse of emergency. She felt in her pockets, hoping she had not imagined it: and there was Frances's handkerchief, pressed into her hands at the last instant, as though for safety. On the way to Cressingdon she had moved it to her face, breathed in, long and deep: she had not known a smell could be this way, lifting her heart and yet soothing it into a long, perfect exhalation. What could she compare it to? She had thought comparisons could fail her, here. But she'd thought of waking with Marina as a child in Spain, so long ago that the memory was only a single picture: a white wall, a wide bed, morning shadows. And a smell: lemons, sun on hot stone, the dry crackle of branches moving in a warm breeze. Comfort and adventure, all in one breath.

Anything could happen if she walked back: another bomb, or – somehow more likely-seeming – a strange man leaping from the hedgerow. And yet – and yet. She looked up at the black sky, the air now fresh and clean, something cleared – horribly, terribly – but cleared nonetheless, as though the sky too had been burnt through, leaving a gap, a moment of possibility.

When she arrived at the cottage it was entirely dark and silent, the low call of an owl the only sound for miles. Ivy could hardly believe that there were three small girls inside. That Frances was there. She lit a candle to carry, crept up to the girls' room, half-expecting to find them awake, peering at the windows in alarm. But her daughters were in their usual poses of abandon: hot red cheeks, flung-out arms, their hair in swirls, patterning the pillows. Between Artemis and Baby, Rose: like a curled question mark, contained and cool, her thumb in its usual position between her lips. They looked natural together, these three girls in descending age. *Like sisters*, Ivy thought, pausing as long as she could in the doorway, the candle wavering.

She no longer felt even slightly tired: sleep was something that happened to others, in other kinds of lives. To children. She opened the door to her bedroom cautiously, careful not to wake Frances. And there was the put-up at the bottom of the double bed, used when one of the girls was ill, or occasionally for Ivy to sleep in, if Bear's snoring was particularly bad. But it was empty, the sheets still pulled up tight as Ivy had left them, this afternoon or a year ago, the blankets soft with rest and expectation.

Ivy moved the candle and looked towards her own bed, the

bed where she had lain with her daughters, turning in the night to feed them, where Bear had risen above her, over and over, their love an ordinary act now, like dinner, like sweeping the floor. But here, in this same bed: Frances. She was turned away, her body curled like her daughter's, the blankets dipping at her waist and lifting again at her hips, her shoulders. Ivy set the candle on the bedside table and began to undress: the air was cold, and she thought for a confused moment of the fire, of how it could have built so quickly in the depths of such spring chill. She reached for her nightdress, pulled its rough cotton over her head, felt the relief of the material falling to her feet, across the lengths of her arms. She would sleep beside Frances, and in the morning they would pretend the kiss never happened: it would be lost, as Marina and Angus's paintings were lost, to the senseless, pointless confusion of war, to fires that swept the earth, leaving nothing.

She lifted the blankets and sheet as gently as she could: the bed was not as cold as she had imagined, the heat from Frances already spread across cotton to reach her. Ivy lay still, turned on her side. It was time to sleep, and yet she thought she might never have been more awake, listening to the wind in the tree at the window, the distant call of the owl. In front of her – inches away – Frances was breathing long and deep, her sleep its own place that Ivy imagined she could enter, walk in its dreams and hidden pathways, knowing at last the way another person could think.

Ivy closed her eyes, watching the flicker of the candle

shadowed against the wall. She should extinguish it now. And she really should sleep: she saw again the flames across the studio, the roof lit up as though it was always meant to end that way, an inevitability, somehow, in the way it had bent and buckled in the heat.

In front of her, Frances began to stir – gradually at first, and then turning in one movement towards Ivy, opening her eyes. In the candlelight her face looked even softer, her eyebrows dipped in concern—

You're back? Is everyone – all right?

Ivy nodded, a sad smile forcing its way across her lips.

They're all all right – shocked – but it was the studio – the paintings—

Oh, God. Oh, no. There was a long silence as they both felt it, the colours of paint seeming to swirl around the room with them, their loss almost visible in the gloom. Frances pressed her lips together.

I hope you don't mind – that little bed didn't seem very welcoming—

There was a nervousness in Frances's voice, Ivy noticed, as though she thought Ivy might not want her to sleep here. How little people understand each other, Ivy thought for a moment. And yet – Frances was quiet, continuing to look at her, her eyes hooded in the dim light. There was more in this look, somehow, than in all of the words of their friendship. Ivy knew – so clearly, it was a miracle how clearly she knew – to reach her hands around Frances's chin, to hold her face completely in her hands.

And there were only a few movements – the economy of their touch what Ivy noticed, first, just one long shifting until they held each other, until her breath was in Frances's mouth, and her face on her neck. Until they were surrounded by each other, barely differentiated in their knowing of each other, the long moment when Ivy ran her hands down the length of Frances's body: when she knew she held the whole of the world.

She felt, suddenly, that she must have been very good, at some moment she could not remember, to have been rewarded like this: the dark night surrounding them, their daughters safely sleeping. And if there was a moment – any moment – when Frances ceased to be Joseph's girl perhaps it was this – the studio burnt, Cressingdon never to be the same again. The whole country on fire, the whole universe remade. And in her bed: Frances. Frances, with her hair falling over Ivy's face, Frances, reaching to pull the whole of Ivy's nightdress over her head, Frances, smiling and kissing and smiling again. She is here, Ivy thought to herself, over and over again. This is happening. Frances: the answer Ivy had searched for, all at once, herself and entire.

DAY FOUR

April 1956

THE BUS ROLLED into the day, Ivy's mind high above the world, as though she had become a giantess, a monster, able to see everything. Here was London, spread before her like a picnic, people scattered beneath the greening trees. Ivy thought she would be content to let this bus roll for ever, for her existence to be an eternity of blossom and sunshine, goodness coming from the windows like the sweetness of her daughters' mouths when they were young, when they would still climb on her lap, hold on to her hair. Now, she sat upright, one hand clutching her handbag, the other on the fuzz of the seat beneath her. She clenched her knees together, felt warmth travelling between her thighs, the bus's rattle giving something close to pleasure, a disruption of the journey.

They passed a tree with overhanging branches, some knocking the window as the leaves rustled through its opening, a smell like – what was it like? A fresh sweetness; spring itself, the sap of the new. She closed her eyes, the noise of the city – trundles and shouts, the growl of engines, the bark of a dog – seeming to merge and blend into something close to a concerto. Yes, she was being romantic. But her life had become so quiet. Ivy had known so little silence, ever since childhood, had found her days always accompanied by a certain background hum, if only of the minds of Marina and Angus, Gilbert's constant intellectual structuring, the birds, even the growth of trees all seemed to have their own sound. Then the war, so filled with noise, both private and public: sounds to be waited for, to be feared, others delighted in. Now, her life was drenched in silence, its own element. She had come from a house – the same small cottage, purchased just after the war – where she had learnt to walk barefoot, so her feet did not make noise enough to startle.

Widowhood: the word was somehow elegant, even sylvan, suggesting to Ivy some deep forest, a dappled green glade where the *widow* lived out the rest of her days. It had been two years since Bear had died, and her experience possessed none of these qualities. Widowhood betrayed its own suggestions; it was a dreary place, comprised of barren, square days Ivy struggled to fill. They had sent the girls away to boarding school at eleven and thirteen – Marina had offered to pay quickly, easily, as soon as the extent of Bear's illness became clear. And now the girls were so settled there, their lives reshaped, as Ivy's was.

Alongside the silence: expectancy, as though at any moment the colours of Artemis's old school blazer would fill the kitchen door, sight before sound, then the rush of her daughter; skin and hair, her arms reaching for Ivy or moving away, her satchel on the table, her stretch to a cupboard for a glass. She thought of Artemis's room now, her books in their mute, stubborn rows, her desk chair tucked under her table. And where was she, this creature – a known beauty, at seventeen – who had grown in Ivy's own body? Running on a lacrosse court somewhere, laughing with people Ivy had never met. Hoping to go up to Oxford next October, to St Hilda's, just as Genevieve had predicted. Ivy did not feel like such a grown girl's mother, but what did she expect that to feel like? She had expected solidity, she realized, a sense of being a wall that someone could lean against. But there was nothing solid about her; she was more like an unravelled ball of wool, she thought now, as she lifted her face to the breeze from the open window. She could almost feel them: the threads of her life that hung about her.

After Bear's death Ivy was astonished to realize how many unanswered questions remained in her life. How marriage, despite its complications, had given her a reprieve, in so many ways, from the tormenting mysteries of her youth. It had been a suspended state; a way of not moving forwards or back, of remaining held in a perpetual present. Ivy had felt the last vestiges of her interest in God leaving her when Bear died: such suffering, no glory in it, her husband only an animal in pain, his body a shell after his last breath. And so with Bear's death, God's death – this was the way she had begun to think of it – and in its wake only multiplicity, it often felt, an endless questioning. Ivy had searched, for over a year now, for an explanation of what happened to Joseph. She had even visited a seance, a strange gathering in a dark house one winter evening, loose window frames quaking in the wind. And yet she had heard nothing important, reached no singularity, no single answer. Everything was scattered, proliferating, meaningless.

But – Ivy closed her eyes – this was surely *one thing*, the air and the rattle and the blossom and her own warm feet on the floor of the bus, rising and falling with the road far beneath it. This morning she could not have imagined that she would be here, like this, in a world of happening. She had felt nauseous, in the small rooms of the cottage; her hands had shaken as she buttoned her blouse. The night before, she had lain awake for hours, the walls of the bedroom seeming to press against her. *What am I doing?* she wondered, over and over again. But she could not have known how it would feel, to be in London today: this steady, rising bliss of event, of the day itself, every noise seeming purposeful, even preordained.

The letter had been slipped through her door a few weeks ago, on an ordinary Tuesday, by the same postman who delivered her letters each day, the familiar rise and fall of his step coming towards her, moving away. She had been sitting at the kitchen table trying to arrange her day into a recognizable pattern: some housework, gardening, a visit to Anne and the others. And meals: meals would always break up the time. Toast for breakfast, every bite savoured, looked forward to. And yet: here was the handwriting, spidery as ever, those almost illegible markings Ivy had to peer at, moving closer to the page until they revealed themselves into meaning.

And along with meaning: the smallest hint of a familiar perfume, discernible on the paper. Frances. Ivy had put the letter down.

She curled her fingers with the memory now, as ahead of her Gamages department store loomed its reassuring bulk, its windows bright in sunlight. She had meant to buy the girls a treat, gloves perhaps, something to present at the boarding school on her next visit. She always took a present, but she was not sure why: she could already see how the girls would place them aside after a brief word of thanks, their faces lit up with themselves, with thoughts of elsewhere. Pansy seemed multiple when she was at the school, as though within her uniform she held several girls, was no longer the child Ivy had raised and lived with all those years. At first, she had found it impossible to imagine Pansy brushing her teeth without her, lying down to dream, waking up the next day and running on a field, her hair streaming behind her, motherless. But gradually she adjusted: they both did. She became used to the sight of Pansy – a rounded, cheerful fifteen-year-old – on visiting days, her features blurred by communal living, the cotton of her shirt washed and pressed by other hands. And there were brief visits home of course, when her daughters' doors were closed and Ivy knew they were sleeping beyond them. But this sleep was no longer the endless, forgetful sleep of childhood, Ivy sensed; it was something else: a place with a deeper, unknown texture, a country she would never visit.

She leant forward before she could catch herself, pulled the cord for the bus to stop. Outside, the sun was bright, the black of taxicabs shining. She passed a poster for the countryside, Sussex: her own county, in perfect colours of green and blue. One would not think that just last week some boys had found a used grenade in the woods outside the village. Or that certain veterans still walked around with their minds missing from their heads, their eyes entirely blank. The countryside was restored, it seemed. Almost intact. And where was death, now, in the city? At this moment, Ivy could not see it; it was as absent as God. Death was not in the toddler who held his mother's hand, the plump pomposity of his thighs, it was not in the young couple who walked close enough for their shoulders to touch, in the way Ivy saw the girl dip her head as the boy whispered in her ear. It was not in the clock tower, the church spire, the peeling advertisements for a bazaar. Even on building sites, the rubble glistened, a bird alighting and departing from a partial brick wall, opening its wings to the breeze.

Sometimes, at moments like these, the unravelling felt more like this: an opening, a way to be unformed, endlessly possible. This was midlife, it seemed, and widowhood too: this tipping, this balance between collapse and expectation. *You have plenty of time*, Marina liked to say. She had even mentioned a *charming* man at her gallery, a widower. There was time, Ivy sensed, but not plenty of it. There was, perhaps, enough.

In the gloves section of Gamages, she felt the different fabrics, touching suede and leather and thick cotton. She often thought, these days, of that old, invented phrase of her youth, *the world of objects*. She saw how, in a sense, the simplicity of things had been returned to her, in God's absence, that a glove was only a glove, the depth she had once seen diminished, leaving only a department store, things to buy or not buy, a choice to be made. She must have stood there too long; here was a saleswoman, expectant, poised.

May I help you with anything, madam?

Ivy paused. She was younger than Ivy, in her late twenties perhaps, still with the impatient, striving look of youth, her body like a spring, coiled and ready. Her hair was pinned neatly, and as she tilted her face Ivy could see in the lights that it was a deep, steady chestnut. There was a liquid drop Ivy had become used to, a sense of hollowness in her stomach. The world clarified, and loosened again, as though a lens had been placed over it and lifted. Ivy had wished, for a long time, that every sight of red hair did not do this to her, that she could be released from men's red hair, and red setter dogs, and even a certain shade of fabric that reflected the light in the same way.

No, I'm perfectly all right, thank you.

The girl disappeared as quickly as she had arrived, her neat figure bustling through the racks. Ivy held the gloves she was touching a little tighter, glanced up at the clock. One hour. In a single hour Frances would be in front of her, to look at, to speak to. It had been so many years: perhaps her hair would not be red at all any more but grey, as Ivy's had begun to be, at the temples and the roots. But for now, Frances remained aflame, as she had been the last time Ivy saw her, the image bringing with it, even now, a dulled jolt of pain.

She bought some gloves in a hurry, fumbling at the cash desk: a summer version, crisp cotton, in emerald for Artemis, ocean blue for Pansy. She was keen to leave the department store, she found, to be out in fresh air again. On the street the city seemed to have quickened, to have raised its tempo to Ivy's heart, the sun glinting off the windows of shops, lighting the leaves of trees which danced towards her. The last time she had been in London, a few weeks ago, spring had been dampened by rain, but now it was shining out of every surface, shameless, blazing. Ivy loved how each spring announced itself as a new event: unprecedented, entirely original.

She and Frances had had three years, Ivy reminds herself now. Three summers, three winters. It was enough, surely. And that last golden summer – the war fully ended, her girls growing into more delightful versions of their small selves. And somewhere, always, like a thread of silver – Frances. Ivy knows now it was the most beautiful time of her life. She knew it even then, a rare gift of foresight. Even Marina was happier, painting more furiously than ever before, as though trying to replace all the works lost in the fire. It was strange, as the years passed, to see the way the fire had the opposite effect on her and Angus: for him it had led to a quietening, something subdued for ever. There was no longer a string of young lovers, causing the atmosphere at Cressingdon to tighten and crack – Charles had never returned, and no one had replaced him. And in the early mornings and late evenings it was more often Marina who could be glimpsed in the rebuilt studio, her hair tied high on her head, stepping back to appraise her work.

Ivy had wondered, sometimes, whether her family noticed, if they caught the looks between her and Frances over their daughters' heads, surely not quite *motherly* even to a casual observer. And yet to Ivy there was never anything unseemly about their relationship, never any sense of dinginess or impropriety. She sometimes had to remind herself that she was, in fact, *having an affair*. She was even, occasionally, tempted to simply tell Bear: would he even be angry? She could only imagine a kind of mute disbelief. Certainly in the family there had been nothing more than a pleasure that Frances had returned to them, that in her some small part of Joseph remained, history itself alive in her, moving, laughing, eating Anne's meals around their kitchen table.

Ivy felt now, as she had not felt for so many years, the breaking of the world into two: Frances, and not Frances. Here, in the street: a bomb hole in the city, piles of rubble still uncleared, all these years later. Someone's life, someone's existence, in tatters. The city still marked by death, of course, after all: so many railings missing, terraces with gaps, like children with lost front teeth, everyone said, but they did not give the same sweet ache as those children. There was something too clean, almost surgical, about the spaces now, as though war were only a gap, a break in time.

And apart from the world, from the street, within her: Frances. Ivy had become used to this, in those years after the fire: how the world had divided, into bed and not-bed, skin and touch, an almost infant ecstasy on one side and the rest of life on the other. Such a simple pleasure, Ivy often thought, nothing complex after all but only the sun of Frances's face, rising above Ivy in the bedrooms they shared with their husbands. Bed and not bed, Frances and not Frances – only this sweet binary, a morning when she stepped into the yard and swore she could smell Frances on the breeze, or – more likely – on her own skin. What was this secret, that a lover lived in your pores, was in fact contained within your flesh for as long as you loved them? A possession, Ivy could call it, the way Frances lived as a spirit in her mind, and then in her form – smell, taste, touch – within Ivy's very body.

Several times a day across those years, at ordinary moments, when washing uniforms or stirring a soup, Ivy would react to a memory of Frances's presence, her movements sudden, involuntary: a tipping back of the head, a sudden gasp. Once, Artemis frowned at her, stopped her drawing at the kitchen table: *What's the matter, Mummy?* she had asked, her head cocked to one side. And what could Ivy say? Sometimes she wondered if there was something wrong with her, after all. How did people live, in the midst of such desire? She struggled to see how human civilization had achieved so much – the building of cities and empires, the creation of weapons and technology – when they could only have lived within this: wanting, and not having. Wanting, and having.

Even now, occasionally, a memory would take her by surprise in its freshness, entering one of her days like a flag, a reminder that life had once had colour and sound, love and movement. She managed, mostly, not to think of the winter of 1947: of that ice-bound morning when Frances had walked – heavily pregnant, bundled in layers – all the way over, risking a fall. The house, usually transformed by her presence, was only itself. It was only the kitchen, the teapot with its woollen cover made by Anne. A shining pot. A painting on the wall. And Frances, just another thing in the room. It was moving day – David had another job, in Scotland. They would begin a new life.

It's for the best – Ivy would always remember the way Frances said this, ice formed on the insides of the windows, the very tips of her fingers turned blue.

At the restaurant, Ivy sat outside, the air still warm enough, only the slightest hints of dusk at the edges of the sky. *A very late lunch – or a very early supper*, as Frances had suggested in her letter – *a little place I know in Soho*. Ivy appreciated the defiance of normal mealtimes; she had noticed that time had lost its meaning, lately, the rigid timetable of motherhood broken down. The table she was sitting at had wobbly legs; she ordered a coffee, turning her face against the sun.

They had agreed not to write, but Ivy could not stop herself sending a card on Frances's birthday every year. Frances never replied, though she sent a condolence letter after Bear's death, with a simple, small message: *I am so sorry for your loss. I think of you often.*

Ivy had replied; she even offered, tentatively, to meet, feeling a warm rush of fear as she did so. And three weeks ago, Frances had finally written back; she had agreed. *I often go to London on enquiries about Joseph*, Ivy had written, and perhaps it was this that had changed things. This – their shared Joseph – that had made the world tip and slope as Ivy had always hoped it would, bringing Frances towards her.

She would be here, after nearly ten years of waiting – Pansy had been six in 1947, Artemis eight: Ivy wondered, even now, if they recall seeing her crying, the balled-up hankies stuffed into the sleeves, the eyes that were always dry by the time Bear returned from work. She wondered if her suffering was visible, or only subterranean, groundwater beneath all of their lives.

Ivy was early; she had wanted these moments, to compose herself. To sit, and to wait. Around her, people had filled most of the other tables, lifting glasses and forks in the late sunlight, small dogs at their feet. It was like Paris, Ivy thought, if not for the red buses, the black taxicabs, a certain English, metallic quality to the air.

She had been to Paris with Marina, long before the war, had played with Joseph in piles of pink blossom that floated from the trees like paper. Marina was more relaxed in Paris, Ivy noticed; she said the whole place *throbbed* with art, galleries around every corner. Ivy wondered if the city would still feel the same, if sitting at a café like this was still possible, even more possible than it was in London. She wondered who she would have become, if she had been brave enough to consider going to Paris, instead of marrying Bear all those years ago. Sometimes, she felt that the other Ivy – the life she once dreamt of, before Joseph died – was visible to her: dancing in a show, acting in America. She could see the dust in the spotlights, could taste the bourbon in the bar, the ache of fatigue in her limbs. The other Ivy would have had many lovers, long nights, taxis riding through streets in the rain. Or perhaps she would only have been here, after all: waiting.

The coffee arrived and Ivy took a sip, though it was still too hot, the inside of her mouth turning numb. But now, truly, was it? Yes – *yes* – here she was: Frances herself, walking down the street towards her. Frances walked with her head held straight, so that Ivy, for those moments, could watch her just as she had been in her mind for all these years. A figure to be spun and manoeuvred; never spoken to.

Ivy! Frances waved, finally seeing her, still a distance away. A police horse passed in front of Ivy's view, then a new auto bus, its redness glowing in the sunshine. And she was closer, and closer: she was here.

Ivy. She had only said her name, but Ivy found herself unable to reply. They hugged: Ivy touched the fabric of her dress. She had not expected Frances to smell the same, she realized; it was almost too much. The underneath of flowers, early morning in a strange garden. The end of a peach in the sun. A sudden rush of sense-memory, of mouths and hands, of the way Frances used to say *I want you* even as she held her. Ivy imagined jumping on the passing auto bus, being rushed away, streaming beyond this acuity. It *was* too much, she found, now. Too much was happening, all at once, after so many years of nothing. But they were sitting, now; Frances was calling over the waiter as though it were an ordinary day, asking for tea with lemon, just as she had always taken it. She was leaning back; she was smoking. She held the packet to Ivy.

I've given up – Ivy looked at her own hands, but then she lifted her head. She let herself look. Frances was intact; she was restored. Time was a nonsense, it turned out. For Frances, there was no time. Her hair was exactly the same. Her shape looked entirely unaltered by her second child. If there were new lines around her mouth, Ivy could only think they came with smiling, with the brightness of the day.

Because the sun did shine on, and Frances was smiling at

her. If she was as nervous as Ivy, she did not show it. She was looking with a deep, knowing curiosity – just the way, Ivy thought, you might look at a painting you loved, with a trust in its brilliance.

You look the same, Frances said. Ivy touched her hair; she knew that was not true.

So do you.

Now that she looked again, Ivy could see some signs of the years on Frances's face, a brief constellation of lines at the corners of her eyes when she smiled, a certain deepening of her bearing, a new strength at her shoulders. But nonetheless, she was the same.

The waiter came again; he asked them what they wanted. Ivy was surprised that there was still food, that in these moments they would do something as mundane as eating. She looked at the menu; it seemed indecipherable.

I'll have the soup.

Frances handed her menu to the waiter with a smile.

So will I.

Ivy could not imagine how the rest of the day would proceed; how she would make all the usual movements, catch a bus, find her train. Her bed in the cottage was unthinkable, suddenly: she doubted that it even existed.

When the soup came it was green and thick, like a kind of swamp; Ivy played with it, not hungry. She felt the need to keep speaking, about anything; she described the seance she had gone to, a few months before.

The table actually lifted from the ground! Ivy saw it as she spoke: the draughty house with its cluttered sideboard, the clerks and nurses and officers lifting a wooden dining table with their little fingers. She remembered the darkness of the sky beyond the windows, the faces spectral in reflection, each one pulled apart in shock. She knew her own enthusiasm had something false in it, her story not allowing for the fear she had felt, the keening wind at the cracks in the door frame that had sounded so much like a voice.

Oh, Ivy. Frances frowned, leaving her spoon in her soup. Of course she disapproved. She was a rationalist, always had been. Ivy imagined Frances waking every morning and staring at the ceiling, seeing only plasterwork. When she splashed water on her face, she did not think it a miracle, simply a combination of elements. And yet here she was, a marvel in her own right.

Why are you doing all this? I'm not sure I understand. Frances took a bite of bread, a sip of water; behind her London rushed on; it did not know her, Ivy thought. It lived a life without Frances, just as she did, these days.

I wanted to find out— Ivy looked at her fingers, frustrated that she could not speak as she wanted to. Words were so little, she knew.

What happened to him – to Joseph. Once and for all. She made her voice lift and fall on the last few words, as though to mock them. She found she could not look up at Frances; she had not imagined their meeting this way. In her dreams, people hardly spoke at all. She had seen a wash of colour, a spring day with Frances at the heart of it. Perhaps a kind of dance. She almost laughed at herself now. She was an idealist; Bear had always said so. She could not imagine things as they really were. But Frances was leaning forward; she was taking Ivy's hand.

Her skin was like the inside of a shell, Ivy thought. Like the silk dress of a doll she had had when she was six.

I understand, Frances was saying, her hair blowing across her face. *It's – admirable, actually. I've never even tried to—* She smiled at Ivy, their old smile, it seemed, full of things said and unsaid, a deepening of life itself, of what could happen between two people. How quickly things could change – Ivy felt emboldened, suddenly. She began to tell Frances of how, only weeks ago, she had visited a psychic. It was someone she had seen in a newspaper, of all places, on another silent morning in the cottage. She had told no one she was going, could not seem to stand the change in their faces as the words registered. Once, she had dared to mention the possibility of *spirits* to Gilbert, had seen his smirk slide into a frown of concern. Interest in this kind of thing was a sign of madness, she knew. *Bonkers*, Angus would call it.

She did say – Cynthia, the psychic – she said she saw Bear – he said – that he wanted me to be happy.

Oh, Ivy— Frances looked down. Her eyes were glossy, Ivy saw. *I'm sure that – he would—*

Ivy remembered the living room of the psychic, the

particular atmosphere formed by *eau de nil*, the heavy breath of a gas fire and something else: a herbal undertone that reminded her of the vegetable market in the village, some musky leaf dried for years. The house had looked ordinary, from the outside. A simple terrace in West Hampstead, up a high, winding hill. But she knew the woman in this particular house was not ordinary. *Madam Cynthia*, the newspaper had called her, her wide eyes flashing above the headline: *Lady Who Charms the Dead*. She was of indeterminate age, perhaps fifty or sixty, with the kind of face Ivy recognized from teachers at school, something mask-like about her make-up, another life hidden behind the eyes.

Ivy had dismissed the article, at first; she thought the use of the word *charms* to be particularly distasteful, as though the dead were snakes who could be curled around a stick. And yet she found herself reading again of how Cynthia Jones – her surname was disappointingly pedestrian, Ivy felt – communed with the dead on a *soul level*, through a *spiral* of psychic communication. Her *celestial telephone*, Cynthia called it at one point; Ivy could not help smirking at this. And yet despite her scepticism she had wondered: what would it be, to *speak* to Joseph? To know, finally, what had happened to him? It was like a snowy morning as a child: the white, unthinkable bounty of it.

But it had not been Joseph who appeared to Cynthia that afternoon, as an overweight Pekinese snored under the table, its breath tickling Ivy's feet. She had felt foolish, to have not considered that it might be Bear – so recently departed – who would appear. Wishing her happiness.

He said – he told me to keep my chin up. She laughed, now, a strange, stuttered sound, not born of humour at all. But Frances continued to look at her, her eyes steady.

He always used to say that— Ivy wiped her eyes. She thought now of the times she had seen Bear happy – such earthly visions, sipping wine in the garden, the sun on his face. Throwing an infant Pansy up into the air and catching her as she laughed in that forced, gurgling way of the very young. Ivy tried to imagine a different, spirit-based happiness: he and Joseph having tea on the lawn at a heavenly Cressingdon, their legs stretched on the grass, the sun gentle on their faces. She was not convinced by this vision, but liked it all the same, liked the way she could see all the details of their dress: their buttons and silken handkerchiefs in pockets, the long gestures of their hands. She liked to think – but did not quite believe – that detail of this kind persisted after even death, that all the attention they paid would be remembered.

Frances held her hand tighter as she spoke, their old confidence healed over, their history like something they could stand on, at last, looking far around themselves. There was something psychic, in fact, about the way Frances listened to her, Ivy thought now, as though another dimension opened when they spoke. Even when they disagreed there was understanding there, or a desire, at least, to understand.

So you really thought that it might be – Joseph?

Ivy paused. The next part felt like too much to say, even to Frances. She made herself rush on, quickly.

I just keep thinking – what if he isn't really dead? What if he is just lost, or— her voice faltered. She must truly sound mad now. But no one had been able to say exactly why Joseph's body was not washed up, as others had been over the years: the maid who weighted her pockets with stones up at Bournton, or the little boy – that awful tragedy – who fell in while fishing. *Some anomaly in the current*, she had overheard Gilbert telling Angus. Some bend in the river, some wash of water or wind, and he had been taken out to sea. But these were only guesses.

What if – Ivy made herself say it – *he was washed up somewhere? Lost his memory, or—*

But Ivy – Frances had stopped her, frowning – *it's perfectly possible, didn't they say, for a body never to be found.*

For a moment they were both silent. Perhaps Frances was thinking, as Ivy did sometimes, of Joseph's bones scattered in the sea – lodged in a coral reef, in the body of a whale.

But don't you ever think – what if? What if it really had happened differently – if everything was – another way—

Ivy's words fell like stones in a pond, seeming to take on a new meaning with each ripple, bringing memories to the surface. Not only of Joseph. Of Frances, her arm looped through Ivy's as they walked across a field at night, her touch the only thing holding Ivy to the ground. Frances eating a cake in Ivy's kitchen, her mouth orbited by sugar. Frances laughing that first night they kissed, the sky wide and open around her.

I do think that actually, I think that all the time.

Frances bit her lip. There was a long silence, the rush of the city barely discernible now, the concerto hushed, rumbling, the city dimming into twilight. The tables around them had emptied, a small biplane was leaving a trail through the sunset, its pilot exultant, perhaps, full of purpose.

I was thinking today that I am a ball of wool— Ivy said this now, and Frances did not laugh. She leant forward, chin on her hands, and looked.

Ivy glanced down at her old dress, her scuffed shoes covered over with polish. But it was not this that Frances saw, she felt. What Frances saw was indescribable.

I feel that I am unravelling, somehow – and yet here I am.

Unravelling?

I seem to not know – who I am, any more. If I ever did?

Do any of us?

Ivy smiled, shyly.

With you, the world makes sense, she wanted to say. *With you, I am myself.* But these sounded too like the sentiments of a romantic song her daughter would hum as she twirled around the kitchen, dreaming of some boy. Yet wasn't it the truth? It seemed perfect, suddenly, to be sitting at this table on a busy street, spring in London, the war long over, her children grown. She lifted her spoon to her mouth, hungry at last, but the soup was cold. She ate the bread instead, tearing off soft, small pieces, one after the other, listening to Frances speak.

Frances's second daughter, Maisy, was only nine: Frances was still, for years to come, in the intense period of motherhood in which children need their parents more than their mothers need them, before they move towards the light of adulthood, mothers left in the shadows. Maisy was keen on lacrosse, a *jolly, bouncing girl*, Frances said, so different to Rose, who remained serious, her mind *a tight knot*. She would go to university next year. Frances was busy, volunteering for local community groups with the Women's Institute. Here was the language of family news that Ivy knew so well, was fluent in herself, its terms a concealment of life, rather than its revelation. Of David, Frances spoke the least of all, and Ivy found that she was grateful for it.

To your ball of wool I say wireless – I'm just a wireless now. I transmit other people's voices. Perhaps that's not so bad— Frances let her head fall back now, let the sun shine upon it.

How silly I sound! Empty-brained—

Ivy was shaking her head, though she did not need to. She knew Frances, and when she looked she saw that the city knew her too, the sky parting to reveal ribbons of lavender, mauve, the leaves of trees becoming jewel-like, salutary. These trees shone with Frances, it seemed to Ivy; the sky was a long, restful expression of her mind. They should leave, Ivy knew; they should walk together into this changed world. And, at just this moment, Frances said it:

We could go and hear some — music?

She stirred her coffee with a teaspoon, looked up, straight at Ivy.

There's somewhere we could go — I still have a few hours.

Before what? Ivy wanted to ask — but somehow, even with all their intimacies, she couldn't bring herself to. She didn't want to know, she realized, would defer knowing as long as she could.

Walking together through a square, Ivy and Frances were not as they had been at the restaurant: two respectable women, a wife and a widow, mothers of fast-growing children with shopping bags, sensible shoes. Now, they were the deep, damp green of the leaves, the grass that released its perfume as they walked beside it, the promise of warmer days, the secret growth of life. They no longer spoke as much; instead they were hanging suspended in their own presence, the mystery they provoked in each other.

Frances took Ivy's hand. Ivy remembered this later: how it was definitely, unquestionably Frances who reached out and took her hand, the square an oasis of green watched over by towering beauty, nature hedged by civilization. If anyone saw them, they could be supporting each other, making sure they didn't fall: the ground was uneven. And there was an innocence, a schoolgirlish crush of their fingers together, coming loose and squeezing again, the smoothness of their palms sliding against each other. It was still nothing, still two friends – one married, one a widow – walking together, on a pleasant evening, keeping each other company.

We're here. Frances was leading her down dark steps in an old building, further and further away from the brightness of the evening. Ivy could hear the music already, the clear, buoyant tone of the saxophone reminding her of the distant country of Easter Sunday, all those years ago, Frances twirling, lit up, on Joseph's arm, head thrown back in laughter, hair dipping to the Cressingdon carpet. Ivy looked at Frances again now: the same person, unquestionably, reaching into her purse at the ticket booth, moving into this throbbing room as though she knew it, as though she belonged there. A jazz club; somewhere Ivy had read about, never imagined she would visit.

The room was filled with more life than she had seen for years, the crowd swelling and softening, a surge of excitement visible as a new song began. Ivy looked to the singer on stage, the woman's fingers curled around the microphone, her voice low, pulling, like the drag of the sea. Her lips were a deep, dark red, her dress a silk negligee, tight across her bust. Ivy glanced towards Frances, as though to check that this was permitted, the two of them, in a place like this. But Frances was only smiling, as though the stage-lights were a bright sunshine, and they only children after all, left to wander, with no thoughts of their beds and toys, the domestic places they belonged to. Ivy knew that she could enjoy anything with Frances. They could be anywhere – sitting at a bus stop in the rain – and it would be a pleasure. But to be here, together; this was almost unbearably rich, even decadent. She touched Frances's arm.

Thank you—

For what? Frances was looking at her, unshakeably.

For this—

But Frances only smiled, shook her head lightly. They went to the bar, Frances not asking what Ivy wanted but simply leaning forward, speaking to a young man in a bow tie. Ivy shifted on her feet, feeling shabby in her old coat, relieved when they took their drinks to a velvet-lined booth, where she could shrug it from her shoulders.

Cheers—

Frances lifted her glass to her lips, and Ivy mirrored her, tasting something sharp and pure, a sensation forming at the centre of her forehead, a long golden string pulling her mind towards the ceiling.

Delicious—

Frances nodded with satisfaction, removed her cigarettes from her handbag.

It's called a gimlet.

She offered a cigarette, again, to Ivy, and this time she accepted. Ivy leant forward; she let Frances light it for her, her hand so close to Ivy's mouth, their knees touching – just for a second – under the table, their bodies angled towards the singer. She could feel the room beginning to reveal itself to her, now that she was settled, inhaling and exhaling gently, deliberately, blowing her own plumes of smoke away. The walls seemed to be moving, their deepness softening. She had the sense, as she had on the bus, that this moment was preordained, that this was the only place she could have been, the only way the evening could have taken shape, after all.

Frances turned to her—

I'll admit, I do sometimes imagine it—

Ivy held her breath: she knew this tone, and the way Frances employed it. She knew it meant a turn in the evening, a train on a sharp bend in the track, the lights of a tunnel appearing, suddenly, to meet them.

What if he was alive, after all – if he was here, somehow.

Both of them turned their faces to the crowd, the impossible becoming, in that moment, believable, that any one of the dancing young men could be Joseph. It reminded Ivy of a feeling she had experienced only in a dream, the logic of time reversed, so that coming down one morning to breakfast Bear was alive, after all, rescued from the grave, restored to eggs Benedict, to the fresh orange juice he had so loved, glistening in its glass.

Ivy was grateful that they could, for these few moments, share the thought: *Joseph could be alive.* He could be here, with them. And what would he have wanted? He would be married to Frances, of course. They would have children, a boy and girl, perhaps, buoyant creatures, skipping across the lawn at Cressingdon, fawned over by Marina. Ivy found she felt no jealousy at this: it was abstract, a sunlit image, a little girl with red hair, with Joseph's freckles. A boy frowning at a steam train, as Joseph had, his hair falling in his eyes.

And yet he wasn't here. Only Frances was here, with her children by some other man, time's path leading her away and back again.

And now. After the first sip Ivy had felt that the alcohol was pointless, only a recurrence of a feeling she already had: this ripe abundance, this growing encounter with the world. Here was Frances's knee against hers, again, a longer touch, replicated in her smile, and then her hand, reaching for Ivy's under the table. Frances looked away, towards the singer, their hands out of sight. The two women watched together, such pleasure in this shared view, the singer enveloping them in sound, her lipsticked mouth at the microphone, her long hands lifting and falling as she sang, landing in her hair, curl-ing a strand around her finger. Ivy closed her eyes to feel it fully: an instant of perfect happiness.

And now Frances lowered her chin, brought her face closer to Ivy's, her hair a tickle at her cheek – their lips touched, just for a moment. Ivy looked around, out of habit, though she found she did not care if they were seen. She leant in again, her fingers holding Frances's face, her lips against hers so confidently now, moving as though they had never stopped being together. Frances reached under the table, ran her fingers behind Ivy's knee, her lightness of touch like eyelashes, like laughter. Ivy felt something within her give way, release itself to the night. There was no caring: caring was impossible, even if she had wanted it. She edged towards Frances's ear, her whisper warm.

We could – go to a hotel?

There must have been great bravery in that moment, if there was no drunkenness. It could have simply been Frances's smell – something like a vineyard at dawn, that place in Spain or Italy, she thought now, somewhere she had holidayed with her parents when she was very small, those trains rocking towards valleys where they rose late in crisp sheets, where she had fallen into a swimming pool, the smell like the first morning on earth.

Ivy, I—

Frances moved away, almost imperceptibly, until their bodies were no longer touching. Ivy thought again of that winter morning, Frances's voice as cold as the bare branches that knocked against the kitchen window. Her voice had the same tone now: it was retreat, Ivy recognized with a sick feeling, a pulling away enacted not in words but in register, her voice not speaking of their hidden selves but only the masks they wore, day after day. Ivy barely listened; she heard only fragments mixed with music, sounds without sense.

David – the girls just at that stage—

Ivy found that she could not believe what Frances was saying. She would not believe it. She felt Frances leaving the world, felt her own self, their mingled presence, the whole of the last few hours, dissolving into nothing. Was it nothing? Frances was looking at her watch. The disbelief again. The impossibility of it. To be left like this, a second time—

—*need to meet David at our hotel*—

Who was David? Ivy wondered as Frances spoke. Perhaps he was a magician, a sorcerer. He had always seemed ordinary, when they had come for dinner at the cottage, joking with Bear about wine, or the stock market. He seemed to view the world as a solid entity, himself as an unchanging element; like a rock, Ivy thought with some small satisfaction. Where Frances was practical, he was simply limited. He had achieved the status of a rock through what he called *hard work*, had secured a nice wife and children and a good job, and now he was free to drift, like debris through the universe, never questioning anything.

They left the club quickly, Ivy avoiding Frances's hands as she handed over her coat, refusing to meet her eyes. Their booth was immediately taken by another couple – a young man and woman who swooned into it, not needing to glance around themselves as they fell into the booth, arms and legs already pressed together.

On the street Ivy walked ahead. She wanted to be entirely apart from Frances, from everything. She could drift, as Bear had told her she could, all those years ago. She could *let herself go*, as middle-aged women were meant to. Take up knitting perhaps, despite the fact that she had been thrown out of embroidery class at school. Join the Women's Institute.

At the end of the road was a war memorial, bunches of flowers still grouped around it. Ivy and Frances had both escaped the war intact, compared to so many. They had all their limbs, all their children. But for what? Ivy wondered now. For this: a concrete path, Frances whole and separate next to her, the clack of her heels suddenly loud, wisps of grey visible at her temples. They walked as far as the Tottenham Court Road together, its life continuing as though nothing had happened: people were getting on buses: they were carrying their lives home, heavily, bulking against steamed windows. Ivy imagined their homes; a pot of soup. A baby with sticky hands.

Ivy—

For a moment Ivy thought there was to be some return, a sealing of their fracture, all of the last minutes a mistake, after all. She wanted to return to the city that was filled with Frances, to the trees and sky and grass in her name. But Frances was gesturing away from them, across the street and down a little; she was pointing to a hotel. And there was David, like a mirage, his fedora tipped down against the growing evening wind, a cigarette at his lips.

You could come and say hello—

And it was only now that Ivy shook her head, when her refusal became something that needed to be spoken. If she had not said something, she felt later, she would have been poisoned by it.

I don't want to say hello, Frances. I want nothing less.

Frances recoiled, the hint of a stranger – David, perhaps – showing in her face, that resemblance couples developed over so many years of sharing space. Ivy turned around, back to the careless, impersonal city. Frances was calling her, it seemed, or a bus was putting its brakes on, a high, exhausted noise moving along the pavement. Ivy walked as fast as she could, further and further, almost running, finding herself at last at the entrance to Kensington Gardens, letting herself fall into its darkness.

Ivy had never been alone in a park at night before. It was not scary: nothing could ever be scary again, it seemed. There was something in her veins: a pure, dancing sensation, as when flying in a dream, feeling certain no harm could come to her. But there was no happiness here, only the certainty that she did not care what happened to her, if she was harmed or not. The sight of a tramp loomed ahead of her, tripping over his own feet.

Madam! It's not safe for you here, madam!

A benevolent drunk, beginning to sing now, something about a farmer and his wife. A cow and a dog. Frances had not been her true self, after all, for those hours: that true self was sitting in a hotel with David, at this very moment, raising a martini glass, toasting the future. Ivy saw Frances's legs crossed at the bar, the elegance of her clothes having a purpose now, beyond costume or concealment. She meant to

attract David, to bind him to her, to live in that eternal settled country of marriage, where the sun never rose or set but
floated, still, in the middle of the sky.

For years, Ivy and Bear had been friends who lived
together, good friends who laughed and raised children and
cared for one another. But in their bed, they turned their
separate ways, perched on its edges like pillars, holding it up
with their separate weights. When Bear died Ivy had
stripped the sheets, though Anne had offered to do it. She
had wanted to feel the absence of him, to touch the places
he had lain for so long, the plains and ridges of his suffering.
She had loved him, in her way, in their way; days passing
gently, filled not with themselves but with some broader,
milder version of existence. And when he was unwell she
had pressed flannels against his hot forehead, held bowls for
him to be sick into. He was part of her family, she knew,
though he could not see – had never seen – her hidden self,
the self that Frances saw.

But what use is that, now? Ivy spoke this aloud, to herself,
feeling like a madwoman. Perhaps she should go back to the
tramp, she wondered, ask for some of his booze. Or she
could buy her own: she could get a bottle of gin and check
into a guesthouse, one with yellowing walls and framed pictures of singers with greased-back hair. She could disappear,
could live there for ever, drinking and wasting away the day,
watching the sun rise and lower against the sloping dressing
table. What was wrong with that life, compared to any

other? Perhaps she would prefer to live there – abstracted, suspended – than return to her widowed life of distant motherhood, the cottage still around her.

For now she continued, seeing a bat fly close by, smelling the fullness of night-time take over the park; a set change, a transformation, the green turning to a deep, undersea indigo, the birds returning to their nests. Ivy was tired; she could sit on a bench, couldn't she? She could lie on a bench, for a while? She had eaten so little: she no longer seemed to have the energy to make it even to the guesthouse, to her escape plan, her non-life of drink and slow breathing. She walked a few more steps, thinking now of finding somewhere hidden in the trees where she could simply lie down. There was still no fear, only a great, lifelong fatigue. She had been wrong, it seemed, to think she had enough time left, for a whole other life.

It would be cold tonight, the wireless had announced this morning. But she had her jacket, and a woollen hat in her handbag. Her hands were numb in a radiant, distracting way: the cold around her head felt like the emptiness of space. Through the trees Ivy saw that she had almost reached the other side of the park, a residential street visible, houses lit with lamps and family dinners, bookcases and carpets and a dog barking somewhere, alone. Closer by, just at the entrance to the park, a church, Gothic, imposing, some of its windows lost to bomb blast. It was not Sunday, but the windows were lit up nonetheless, a few strains of organ music discernible on the breeze.

At the church's entrance Ivy smelt incense, felt parts of herself soften and fold, return to themselves. It was a childhood smell, she realized, from rare days at the village church, even rarer mornings with her grandmother Emily, pressed next to her enormous skirts, the priest parading like a bat down the aisle, the solidity of his black cassock as he chanted in Latin, his back turned to them. The smell had made Ivy feel that she was on a tremendous adventure, the world dividing into parts she had not seen or imagined, unthought expanses of faith and mystery. There was more, she had realized, than painting and galleries and notices. More than the atmosphere in the studio, the stilled egotism of great minds, the staggered movement of their expression in paint. There was more, even, than endless nights laughing in the garden, the grass rolling to the river, the night soft and benevolent above her.

But when they left the church the day always seemed ordinary, lit not by divinity but by a weak, springtime sunshine. Grandmother Emily had bundled her into a café where they ate dripping sandwiches, sipped sugared tea. Life was this, after all: decorators and policemen hunched over soft white bread, eggs and sausages on floral plates. The world didn't know that there was more; perhaps, truly, there wasn't.

Now, Ivy stepped into the church, only at this instant feeling the cold enter her body, though she had been outside for hours. Someone was playing the organ, its music

peopling pews that were otherwise smooth and empty, waiting with the endless patience of religion. Ivy was tired; it was
as good a place as any to sit down. She wondered why the
tramp was not sitting here, why the whole tired mass of
London could not sit here, rather than bustling and rushing
as they did. She thought of Frances, lifting a bite to her
mouth, eating and drinking as though those moments in the
club – even Ivy herself – did not exist. She saw David again,
his hat ringed with street light, the tilt of his nose as he bent
to his cigarette. He was at ease, she had seen; he knew his
wife would come back to him, it seemed: he was expecting
it. Of course he was; he suspected nothing. There was nothing, in fact, to suspect.

Ivy sank her body on to the solid wooden bench, cast her
eyes to the altar by habit. There was Jesus, the same everywhere and new each time, the curve of His ribs, the slant of
His thigh bones, so boyish, almost feminine, the plaintive
cast of His arms, flung above His head. There could not be
a single person, Ivy thought, who in this society was not
compelled by His nakedness. Outside on the street people
were at such pains to cover every one of these features, and
yet here they were: His toes, with their particular shape, His
underarms. *The underarms of God.* Ivy smiled despite herself,
shifted in the pew: she had never been able to avoid jokes in
church. The whole place seemed to ask for them, though
there remained that metaphysical insistence on seriousness.
In the Bible Jesus never laughed, Ivy remembered Reverend

Giles saying to her once. And yet how could that be? Surely any God who was human would have to laugh.

There was a candle flickering on the altar, a distant light in a side chapel, another on by the porch. The church was held in a soft stillness, the rush of London like life seen from the moon, barely relevant. The organ continued, something slow that reminded Ivy of rain, of days inside with water lashing at the window. She folded her hands in her lap, tried to follow the music. She should get her train. And yet no one was waiting for her. For the whole of the rest of her life, no one would be waiting for her. It was a thought that, when her children were young, would have exalted her. Back then, she rejoiced in a quiet house, in the silent faces of plates beside the sink, the divine peace of a flapping white sheet in the breeze. She thought of her prayers in the privy, over the porridge pot: were they only an anaesthesia? she wondered now. Some women resorted to gin, and Ivy looked to God. Her life had been so noisy then: all she had wanted was silence.

Without Frances, her life seemed a flat plain, unbroken by trees or houses, any feature of interest. Once, as a child, she had driven through the fens with Gilbert and Joseph: they were visiting Cambridge, some college or other, and then Ely, for the architecture of the cathedral. In the countryside between, Ivy had seen the horizon stretched as far as it could go, a stark emptiness above, an endlessness of sky. This was the landscape of her future, it seemed: no horror, only a certain plainness. Perhaps it would not be so bad. Here were her hands, as limp and useless as those of Jesus above her. Here was the warm wetness of her own tears, falling against them. She felt the strings unravelling, the many parts of herself loosening, dropping without purpose. Now, she was not even a dilettante. She was truly nothing, at last. She thought again of the room in a boarding house: perhaps a man could come there, into her room, into her bed, removing all thought. She imagined his hot breath against her neck, the dampness of his undershirt against her skin. The room would be blanched by the act, numbed by it, her headscarf thrown over a lamp. Nobody would need to know.

There was a creaking: the organ had stopped. A tall, stooped figure appeared at the front of the church, began walking towards the vestry. He looked up, briefly, taking in the church as one sweeps an empty field with the eyes, expecting nothing. There was only the slightest hesitation as he took in Ivy, his pace neither slowing nor changing its rhythm. Then from somewhere nearby she heard voices, a door opening and closing. She thought of the vestry at the village church, the few times she had seen it: piles of prayer books, the priestly robes hanging like any other garment. A teacup. A hairbrush.

Two people emerged from the direction the organist had gone, began busying themselves with something at the altar, then arranging chairs in a circle around it. There was a small, elderly priest, his gait shuffling, his spine curving his head to the ground, and a round, lively nun, a little older than Ivy, in a blue smock, a headdress that fell down her back. From where she sat, Ivy could watch them without a sense of being watched in return, as though they were performing, and she their only audience. Despite their different postures, the priest and nun carried themselves with the particular decorum of the church, movements that were not quite holy in themselves, but seemed to aim only for the avoidance of offence. What was this, Ivy wondered, to spend one's life in not giving offence? It was a kind of withdrawal, it seemed to her now. An avoidance of truth.

They finished their task, and Ivy found that she was disappointed: she had not wanted the play to end. While it lasted, she had not thought of the plane of her life: she had not thought at all. The priest shuffled back to the vestry, but the nun began to walk down the aisle, a large wooden cross bouncing on her chest. Ivy prepared to nod and smile, she could manage this, at least. But the nun paused when she reached Ivy's pew—

May I?

There was no option to refuse. She thought of the boarding house, of the man she had imagined, the smothering, meaty weight of him. If she could do this, she could speak to a nun. She nodded.

Please—

The nun sat down on the pew, close to its end, leaving a wide space between them. She closed her eyes, and breathed deeply. Was she praying? Ivy wondered. It seemed a strange gesture, to come and pray next to a stranger. Ivy thought of standing, of excusing herself. But she would have to pass the nun, press herself against her, or make her stand. She couldn't do this; politeness prevented her. Instead, she closed her eyes. She could smell the nun beside her: incense and flowers, and something else – the laundry of a nunnery, perhaps, a high, clear cleanness.

It had been a long time since Ivy had prayed, and where once there was a clearing, a swept-clean place in her mind, she found only a jumbled darkness, peopled by demons. There was Bear's suffering, and the stretched skin that separated her from her children. There were the lips of Frances, and their closure on a glass, at a bar where she drank with her husband. There was a kiss, the pressure of the air between their lips, the noise Frances had made as they pulled apart, a small O of surprise, or wonder. Ivy opened her eyes. That was no prayer: it was torture. She was crying again, she realized with irritation. She started to gather herself to leave, politeness be damned. But the nun was opening her eyes too: she turned to Ivy with a look of keen curiosity, a certain lightness in her eyes, her forehead pulled tight by her headdress.

Is everything all right?

Ivy laughed; she could not help it. *Is everything all right?* Nothing was right; it had not been right for a long time, if it ever had. Here she was, in the middle of her life, and could she ever, just once, have said that everything was all right? Perhaps with Frances, though it had been a secret all along, and now was lost for ever. Or: an image came to her of a summer meadow, lying with Joseph in a thin cotton smock, grasses scratching her back. *I'm happy*, he had told her. And Ivy had wondered: was she happy? Now, her eyes filled again. She looked at the nun.

I'm sorry, I have to—

But she did not move. She placed her hands in her lap, helpless.

I'm Edna. Sister Edna.

Ivy. She sniffed, wiped her eyes, cross with herself.

There'll be a service in a few minutes. You're most welcome to stay. It's our Maundy Thursday liturgy this evening.

Maundy Thursday. Of course. It was almost Easter, the anniversary hovering, as it always did, a perceptible change in the quality of the air, as though the whole world knew when Joseph had died, was adjusting itself accordingly.

I have a train to catch—

But again, she did not move. There was a long silence: Ivy could hear the church doors opening and closing, saw people in long spring coats move past her, towards the chairs at the altar, the organ beginning again. Ivy could feel Edna's gaze upon her, some watchful benevolence that felt familiar, as though she read of it long ago, in a storybook.

Bless you. Jesus cries with you, Ivy.

There was a pause; Ivy did not look up, but imagined

Edna bowing, or making some other holy gesture, her hands pressed against the soothing blue of her smock.

You are God's beloved child.

And with that she was gone. Ivy watched as she joined the circle of chairs at the altar, her gait slow, unhurried, unaltered by her interaction with Ivy: why wouldn't it be? She would leave, Ivy decided. Take the train home, after all, submit to the silence of her life, the cool unfolding of her days. It would be bearable: she could bear it. But she found she could not move; the service began, and still she did not move. The priest – this small, stooped man, who reminded her somehow of Gilbert – rose to read the psalm, his voice quavering in the still air.

I love the Lord, because he hath heard my voice—

Ivy closed her eyes: there was something about these words, their forms following tracks already laid down, years ago, other services attended with her father, his suited body bulked against hers, his knee jumping nervously, as it always did.

The sorrows of death compassed me, and the pains of hell gat hold upon me: I found trouble and sorrow.

Ivy let herself cry again: there was pleasure in this, she found, the only kind left to her now: of relief. She let the tears roll down into her mouth; she tasted their salt.

I will walk before the Lord in the land of the living.

She lifted her handkerchief to her eyes, dabbed gently. The psalm was ending and she felt, suddenly, that she was being rude, sitting away from the group, that gentle-looking circle. There were a number of empty chairs, and she moved forward into one, sitting just as the priest rose to read the Gospel, standing again to follow suit. Only Edna raised her head to smile at Ivy; the rest tactfully looked away in that particularly English way, something tender in their disregard. She wondered what she looked like; undoubtedly tired and crestfallen after her odyssey of a day, the heels of her shoes even further worn than they had been in the morning, her slip falling below the hem of her dress. But perhaps – she hoped – she had remained herself. Ivy. Intact, somehow.

The priest's voice was too loud, as priests' voices tended to be, as though he was speaking to a whole crowd, rather than a gathered few—

After that he poureth water into a bason, and began to wash the disciples' feet—

Ivy could see the others around her beginning to loosen their shoes. She felt glad that she had only worn cotton socks, and not stockings that day, though earlier her legs had been cold, a feeling that reminded her of wartime and childhood. She did not want the priest to wash her feet; she never wanted it as a child, either, but she had submitted to it, as she would now. It reminded her of being a young mother, and wishing to break a limb, or be taken down by a mysterious illness that would require her admission to hospital, a break at last, but not one she had to arrange or engineer in any way. There was no choice; this was what mattered.

The priest was kneeling now: his gestures looked almost perfunctory, on the feet of others, the curled toes of the smart businessman, the nobbled ankles of an elderly woman. But when he came to wash Ivy's feet she found his touch inexplicably soothing, her foot lifted by another hand, the warm water poured across it. She was so rarely touched, now. Widowhood was like girlhood, in this way: those long stretching days of loneliness before her marriage.

The priest had finished now, leaving her feet wet, glistening in the cool church air. She thought of the days to come, the long Good Friday service tomorrow, followed by the pause on Saturday: the moment of stillness before the world once again erupted into hope, flowers on the altar, chocolates for the children. The year before Joseph died Gilbert had stayed with them, had made Ivy and Joseph accompany him to church on Easter Sunday, leaving the house to its preparations for lunch. Ivy, having protested, found herself touched by the new flowers, the spring light in its patterns on the warm white walls. Joseph had been half-asleep, yawning with stale breath until Gilbert poked him in the ribs, made him sit up straight again. Joseph had listened, or appeared to listen, while Reverend Giles read of Mary Magdalene finding the empty tomb, that moment of running elation as she fled back to the disciples to tell them the news. Ivy thought, now, as the priest washed the last person's feet, of that stumble through morning air, thousands of years ago, the air electric with the impossible.

She thought of Cynthia, of the silence after she had asked if Joseph was there. A strange thought entered her mind, like a dream-thought, wavering with its lack of logic: who could say, absolutely for certain, that he had not been resurrected? Mary had not recognized Jesus, as the gardener, until she saw Him. What if Ivy had met Joseph, countless times, and failed to know it was him? She shook her head: she was very tired, she told herself. These thoughts were simply biological aberrations, the product of fatigue, depression, the hormonal shifts of her body. But though the thoughts could be dismissed, the feeling remained: Joseph was with her, it seemed. He was in everything.

God so loved the world, that he gave his only-begotten Son . . .

Lift up your hearts.

We lift them up unto the Lord.

Ivy found herself saying words she thought she had forgotten; it was easier to speak than not to speak: she let herself be carried, her mouth moving, making the shapes it had been accustomed to.

Holy, holy, holy, Lord God of hosts . . .

It was the same tune that Reverend Giles used at this point in the service: Ivy felt her voice warble and rise to join the thin tone of the small congregation. And when they shifted and stood for communion she followed them: she knelt at the altar, her hands outstretched. Here was the body of Christ, pressed into her hands by the priest, dry and unyielding in her mouth. And here was Sister Edna, leaning down with the large silver cup, her bearing somehow like an angel, a beam of light from a passing car catching the high lines of her cheekbones. Ivy smelt her again: that laundry purity, the wash of forgiveness. *Given for you.* She looked up, and her eyes met Edna's, the bright intelligence there, the true kindness.

Amen.

Ivy took the cup in her hands, felt the intricacy of its making against her skin. She placed her lips around its edge – here were Frances's lips around her glass, here was her head tipping back – and let wine flood her mouth. It was more than she had ever drunk at communion before, a swell of richness. There was a deep, thick darkness as she closed her eyes, the busyness quite gone now, a radiating swell in its wake. She stayed kneeling, feeling some dark, glowing ecstasy build within her, travelling from her legs to her pelvis, across her stomach, into her hands. She feared she would fall backwards. She feared that she would not. She was held, instead, as though by a cord in the flow of a dark river; here, her selfhood was pure, without feature, thousands of years old. *You're simply yourself.* She heard the words of Bear, echoing from another lifetime. And into this moment: light. The light she had seen on that distant Easter Sunday, returned in a new form. Here was life, silent and speaking. Here – after everything, was peace.

DAY FIVE

April 1965

SHE WAS WOKEN by the bells. Three peals of three, Trinity within Trinity, thirty-three, every year of our saviour's life. It should have been familiar by now, this sound that began every one of her days. But there remained – even after years – this contrast between her dreams and the sound, the life of her unconscious, and the nunnery that surrounded her. There was always this transition, between the surging, layered life of sleep, and the simple partitions of her days. It was five-fifteen in the morning, the time she had woken every day for the past three years, and yet the light still seemed alien to her, not the light of the sun, but of some other, far-off star.

She was held in her cell, for these seconds: Ivy allowed herself ten before she stood up, luxuriated in them, stretched them, lived within them. She watched the concertina of the curtain that divided her from the other cells, from her Sisters, who she could hear waking themselves, their beds squeaking, their bodies sighing, letting out air. Once the ten seconds were over Ivy had learnt that it was easiest to get up immediately, not to prolong the reluctance. It was like having babies, in this way: the sharp alarm of necessity, the need to continue without questioning.

Ivy sat up in the plain white space, a quartered square of early sunlight already present on the floorboards. It was easy to believe in God, on these mornings: He poured through them, the whole cell a glowing egg of light, the simple jug on the night stand, resting on its basin. Marina would think this beautiful, Ivy knew. It was like a painting by one of her friends, the surly woman who always depicted monastic-looking bedrooms, a single flower in a vase. Ivy got out of bed and knelt beside it, her knees meeting the rough strands of the wicker mat. She could feel the contact making its patterns, maps that would appear and fade, different shapes each day. She prayed, her lips against her own cool skin, the darkness behind her eyelids blooming. At these times she didn't reach for God: sometimes He was there, like a fish risen from deep waters, and sometimes there were only the waters themselves: anonymous, undulating.

She got up, splashed cold water from the jug into the bowl and across her body. She was nearing fifty, her body finished with its cycles and waiting, its swelling and deflating, the endless hope of new life. She was only herself, now, and sometimes felt like a girl with it: the calendar horizontal, continuing, no more peaks of emotion, the inevitable descent into blood and cramps. She was strong and solid, from the digging and lifting and sweeping of her days, her arms and legs hard with muscle. She heard the others splash, the same splashes as every morning, the repetition holding holiness within it. She had seen the way that God rose against stillness, as a bird will, appearing when life is taut and constant, its watchers held in their hide.

She pulled on her undergarments, the long rough cotton of them hardened and wasted in places from so much washing. They were fresh: a smell of the laundry, a scent for ever bound with her first months at this convent on the coast, days when she felt so alone and so devoted, the pale hang of the sheets from the ceiling racks, the way light poured through them like wings. *Get up*, Sister Xavier would say, when she sank to the floor in prayers of thanksgiving. *Get on with your work.*

She lifted the tunic over her head, those brief moments of darkness that seemed, even now, like a game. *You be the horse*, Joseph would say when they dressed up. *I will be the knight.* And what would he think of her now? She smiled to imagine it, the way he would pull on her scapular, lift the cincture and let it fall again. A nun! She turned her neck before lowering the coif, preparing for the way it would seal her in her own mind, her hearing muffled, her sight obstructed. That crackling, rushing sound of the linen, like holding a shell to your ear. She remembered how perfect this seemed at first, how much she longed to be separated from the world. Then how she hated it, cursed it, and now, finally, its banality. She no longer had the qualities of the human animal, could not sense threat from the corners of her vision, as nature had evolved over so many centuries to do. But there was no need: there was no threat here.

She stood against the curtain, her last moments of solitude before she joined the community, remained there, her selfhood blended and merged with her Sisters, the whole of them forming a second self, a single entity that kept the place lit and fed and turning: a machine of prayer, Mother Superior said to her in her first year. A mechanism of the divine.

In the hallway, light fell from each of the high windows across their bodies, each figure a drape of fabric, the folds themselves seeming to hold some depth of the universe, their smooth solemnity like the rings around planets she had seen in books in the library. It was fascinating to her, still, how many priests were amateur astronomers, how many looked for God in the sky.

She joined her Sisters walking across the cloister, each archway perfectly symmetrical, the heavy soles of their shoes breaking into sound on the stones. It would always be striking to Ivy how certain noises came to signify the pattern of a whole existence, how for so long afterwards this rhythm would speak to her of duty, and silence, of the hushed intention of so many women moving together, seeking the Lord. The building was designed for God, Ivy always thought, was meant in its construction to echo His movements, to be His body in the world. No wonder it was easy, as they moved into chapel, to feel the reality of the divine, in the soar of the ceiling, the wave of the candles, the light through stained glass hazed and lingering, like a second dawn.

She took her usual pew, knelt on the hassock embroidered with a long-gone date. Some saint's day, an anniversary so fresh and now faded, the threads beginning to fray. She propped her hands against the wooden railing, the movement barely thought of now, though once it had been awkward to her, almost unnatural. Sister Dominic stood to begin the office, her large hands around the prayer book, her wide shape almost a silhouette against a high, arcing window.

O Lord, open thou our lips—

Ivy felt her breath leaving her body, a deep exhale that seemed to ebb into her Sisters around her, to form part of their bodies, their own breath meeting hers until they were truly one body, a single breath at worship. For the first time in years, this would be her only office in the chapel today. She would not be present for Terce, or Vespers, or Compline. The sun would move around the chapel unseen by her: the trees would rise and fall with their murmuring. The thought made her feel briefly, abstractly panicked, as though she had forgotten something important. In this life, with its ebb and flow of God, the routine itself sometimes seemed the clearest sign of Him, the thing that never changed. Ivy still did not understand why God came and went, but she had found a way to live with it, within it. She wondered, sometimes, if it was she, all along, who was absent, rather than Him. *Know God by His creatures*, she remembered, and she tried: she saw the divine in the gardens, in the vital run of a squirrel, the steady pecking of a bird. In her Sisters, their moods and exhalations, their irritations, slowness, boredom and suppressed anger. And today – just for today – she would leave it all.

The telegram had come after supper a week ago, the convent already moving towards the great silence, the quiet seeping into the dining hall like a mist that slowed their movements, made them turn their eyes to the windows.

MARINA WORSENING. COME WHEN YOU CAN.

Somehow, in these six words, Ivy could sense Angus, could hear his voice through the soar of the capital letters, his stare in every space between them. There had been another missive, months before this, and Ivy had rushed to Cressingdon only to find Marina sitting in bed eating toast and marmalade, asking what all the fuss was about. That could happen again, she knew. Marina had continued to send her letters, though lately they had been dictated to Anne, and only signed by her – a single, scrawled line. And their content had narrowed, from general discussion of village affairs, weather, housekeeping, art world gossip, to a single subject: Joseph. Marina had become, at the end of her life, preoccupied with Joseph's death as never before. She wanted to know everything that Ivy had discovered – *during all your explorations*, as she put it. Angus had even confided to Ivy, on a muffled telephone line one late evening last winter, that Marina had claimed to see Joseph, from time to time, that he had simply appeared at Cressingdon, as he used to, wandering around the kitchen stealing scraps from the counters, or hitting a shuttlecock with his old racket in the garden. She was confused, Angus had said. *Not herself.*

As she read the telegram Ivy had felt the remaining Sisters – those who lingered over their rice pudding, the dregs of their tea – turning their eyes upon her in that particular, tacit way they had, as though not really looking at all. She had stared at her saucer, the perfect circle of it, a cool space she could lower her head to, she thought, if nobody else was around. But she would not be alone for hours: there was Recreation, and Compline, and bathing before, at last, the grateful sink into sheets and blankets.

She always fell asleep so quickly: there was rarely any time to think. But that night she lay awake for hours, her mind snagged on the same moment, pulling at it as though it was a thread caught on brambles, a toy in the mouth of a dog. The last time she saw Marina before she fell ill: years ago, the fall of evening light across the kitchen table at Cressingdon, Marina's face curled in disgust. *A nun? For God's sake. I know you've taken Bear's death hard but honestly—* The way she had managed to dismiss Bear and God in the same sentence; there was something so painful in it that Ivy had felt the world dim for a second, as it had when she was so much younger. She had not explained anything to Marina, in the way she had tried to with her daughters. She had not lain her faith out on the table, like a piece of rare jewellery. *Pearls before swine.* This is the phrase that came to her now, though Marina was surely the least porcine of people.

Now, Ivy moved forward to the railing for Communion; her Sisters were singing, lifting the corners of the chapel like a bed sheet, causing the whole place to billow and wave with their beauty, the unity of their voices in candlelight, surrounded by incense. She knelt down: she knew it could be dull, like so many others, the wafer chalky in her mouth, the wine no more than a gulp of acidic juice. *We do not ask for daily miracles* – so Mother Superior was always saying. *God is not fireworks.* But as Sister Peter bent over her, Ivy prayed, nonetheless, for something that would give her strength, for this day, for all that lay ahead of her.

Her prayer was answered, it seemed: the bread felt like life itself in her mouth, something firm and present in its passage across her tongue, her teeth, her throat. And then the wine: she held herself firm, for a second, feeling unready. Then let herself fall: into the realms that were lifting for her, the folds, a formation of petals, an opening into radiance and bliss. Into perfection.

How could she ever explain this to Marina? she wondered, as she knelt in her pew afterwards, her hands pressed and warm in thanks to God. She could say it was like the climax of love, she supposed, although Marina would be embarrassed. And worse: she would be unconvinced. Why go to church, Marina might ask, if love gives just the same feeling? The love of God is infinite, Ivy might say. It is everything. Perhaps if she compared it to paint, to art itself – it is the brush, she could say. The canvas. But it never ends.

For breakfast, the dining hall was filled with sunlight, the walls seeming to expand with its glow, as though the whole place were a lantern, about to rise from the ground. Ivy thought of the young postulant who told her that she often felt she was swimming in God, rising and falling through His beauty. Ivy had blinked at her, rearranged herself on her chair. She knew her eyes were filling, thinking of the river. Of Joseph, and her younger self, almost a stranger to her now: that girl who swam towards a distant light, not knowing it would change her whole life. When she first came to the convent she asked Mother Superior if the light on Easter Sunday had been God; Mother answered that all light came from God, that God was *the ground of all being*. She had patted Ivy's hand, an unusual intimacy, sensing, perhaps, the gravity of the moment. *God is in all things, Ivy.*

There was porridge today, which made her think of her daughters, of the way they would smear it around their faces, how she would find it later, dry and segmented in their hair. Ivy had always struggled to keep her mind in this place, as they were taught, to breathe into each moment. She thought of her daughters several times a day – on some days, it seemed she never stopped thinking of them. And today she would see Pansy, her youngest child, at Cressingdon. They had letters, brief visits at the convent. But to see her in the world was much rarer – Ivy realized she was not touching her porridge, though the others around her ate hungrily: all of them had already been up for hours. Sister Michael was looking at her, she noticed, a small smile on her own dry lips, her spoon in mid-air. She was Ivy's favourite, though they were not meant to have favourites, were meant to love each of their Sisters with *agape*, a pure, Christ-like love. But – Ivy thought mischievously sometimes – wasn't there one disciple in particular whom Jesus loved? Were they truly meant to be more perfect than He was?

Sister Michael painted watercolours on fine days, walking up the hill with an easel and a wooden box that she opened at her feet. Ivy had found ways of going up there, glimpsing the works as they spread across the canvas. *Sister Francis*, Sister Michael always greeted her as she walked by, *what brings you here?* And Ivy always said nothing, just continued on her way. She loved how the world looked from the hill above the convent: spread out, as though God Himself could lie across it, as He seemed to, many evenings, the hills and sea deepening with presence.

There was one particular night, soon after she had arrived at the convent, when she climbed the hill by herself after supper. It was a still evening in early autumn, the sun beginning to set across the horizon, the sky pinking and softening, the skin of the world seeming pressed and moved by God, until it fell into a shape of perfect beauty. The colours were like the most vivid film she had ever seen; there was a sense of the earth holding goodness and wonder, of life there, excitement. There was also, unexpectedly, a great sense of freedom, as though Ivy could fly, as the birds did, dipping from mountain to sea, or at least continue to exist in this: a place of love. Though there were many days after this – of reading, praying, discussion with her elders – Ivy knew that this was the moment she decided to stay. To become some-one else.

She had chosen Francis for St Francis, lover of nature and children, but of course she had thought of Frances, of the letters she still received, once a month, sometimes more, that particular handwriting that was still the most exciting text she knew. They had begun to arrive shortly after she entered the nunnery – *I do not expect a reply*, Frances had written, and for a while Ivy did not write in return. But still the small envelopes arrived, with their folded notebook pages within them, and one day Ivy began to answer, gently at first, almost politely: details of the weather, news of her girls. She kept Frances's letters in the pockets of her habit, sometimes for days at a time, often unopened, exuding a warmth that seeped across her leg, her middle, that sat within her, waiting.

I'm so sorry, Frances had written once. *It was cruel of me, to give hope and take it away—*

I forgive you, Ivy had written to Frances, in return. At

night, she worried that she had lied, in writing this. But it had been all she could say.

She only ever opened the letters alone, in the minutes after waking or before sleep, had found she was able to memorize them, to pass the words over herself when she was in the kitchen or the laundry, her hands in soaped water. She felt guilty for this, of course: she prayed for forgiveness, for the will to think of Psalms, instead, as she worked. But was she not devoted? Did she not love God? In the depths of the night, the thought came to her that she was not sinning at all.

On the train Ivy found it hard to remain in her seat, in her body, her mind leaving her to roam across the landscape, to rest in a hedgerow, to climb the peak of a hill. When she boarded, she was conspicuous, of course, blazing in her headdress against the dull iron of the train, the worn material of the seats. Men made themselves feel good by taking her luggage, getting her settled, asking her if she needed any-thing more. Children pointed to her head, whispered loudly to their mothers behind sticky hands. Ivy should have been used to it: she had left the convent before, had travelled wearing her habit. But it was a warm day: her coif felt more restrictive than secure. Somewhere, below the cotton, her head had begun to itch.

And then, when the train moved, a breeze moved over her,

such a blessing that she closed her eyes, felt only the coolness on the skin of her face, the warmth of the sun through the window. When she opened her eyes, the other passengers seemed to have receded, further away now, their looks and whispers no longer her concern. Her whole vision was taken by what she could see from the window, the unfolding of fields, houses where entire families lived, a whole city visible from a bridge. She could feel the world opening, her own heart seeming to open with it, to spiral into the waiting present. *I am alive*, she felt. *I am here.* The train carried on, such a regular rhythm: she did not have to force it, to use her own will at all. It was how they should be with God, Mother Superior said: submissive, accepting, not relying on their own power or judgement. Ivy saw her day laid out before her: this train, and then another, to the green, familiar world of Cressingdon. To Marina. She saw each part in her mind, flat as a child's drawing. She tried to lift each one to the day's beauty, to give every encounter to Him.

As they neared London, the train began to slow, running beside rows of houses, so close she could see the details of bookcases, torn curtains, a child playing against a fence. At the station, she waited until everyone had left the train and stepped out slowly, the cathedral-like roof rising above her, its smoked newness reminding her of another life, of new life: the outside world, that had continued all this time without her.

★

She had to change trains now, to get from Waterloo station to Victoria; she could have taken the Underground, of course, but preferred to walk, accepting glances from strangers in return for people, movement, the life of the city. Ivy took a deep breath: the day was thickening with exhaust and cooking smells, an auburn fraying at the edge of her sight. London had changed since the last time she had visited, just two or three years previously, and so much more since she had spent time there during the war. The smells were different now, the colours, the fabrics and vegetables that lay outside the stores that she passed. People dressed differently, they were from countries all around the world. She watched a couple walking ahead of her: the man with long hair, a luxuriant beard, the woman with equally long hair tied in plaits, a miniskirt that barely covered her modesty. The girls had tried to keep her informed: of the new Labour government, the new music – they were both enormous Beatles fans – but she felt that she could not keep up, somehow. There was a looseness to life now, a great unsealing. And here she was, wrapped up tightly, damp with sweat beneath her habit. She walked along the river and was grateful for the breeze, for the wide stretch of it, its small waves caught in the sunlight.

Past the river, she looked around at the street signs; she told herself she had not realized she was so close, though she had looked at the address so many times, in the sender box on the back of each one of Frances's letters. Frances – her whole person, her whole body and life – was only streets away. *Come and see me*, she had written, over and over again in her letters. *Or can I visit you?* But Ivy had made no plans for either. *It's not permitted, sadly*, she had written in her last letter, a simple lie – visitors were welcome, on certain days – but one with good reason.

But now she found herself walking in the direction of the address. She would simply look at the house, she told herself, then she could always imagine it when she read Frances's words, the red or blue front door, the colour of the brick. Frances was finally writing journalism again, for some radical political newspaper. She was living here, without David, without her daughters. She and David had divorced a few years ago, *amicably*, as Frances always put it in her letters, the true reasons like a fly around the room, an opaque buzzing that Ivy – even perhaps Frances herself – would never fully interpret. Marriages just ended, sometimes, as other things did. It could not always be explained.

How was it, Ivy thought for the thousandth time, that they had missed each other? After she had seen Frances in London, Ivy realized that for years she had been expecting – foolishly, senselessly – that they would find a way to be together. She had been hoping for it, in truth, without even voicing the hope to herself. It must have been what carried her through, all those long days of Bear's illness, the nursing and cleaning, the meals and tablets carried up, the mess and smell. This was the reason the disappointment was so acute, surely, why her whole life had to be re-formed in its wake, given in an entirely new shape.

But wasn't it curious, she thought now, how much of her life then was similar to her life now, the bending and scrubbing of it, though her drudgery in the convent seemed like the finest craftwork, every clean sheet bathed in the light of God. Back then, with Bear, it was done for love, of a kind, but Ivy had felt, on many days, that she lived in a dark passageway, and that somewhere, very far off – so far she could not even see it – was happiness.

And here it was, of a different kind than she had imagined: she had given herself to God, at last. It was what He wanted, she told herself. It was her calling. Her way of making amends, if nothing else. Of living a good life. But now, here was Frances, living as an unmarried woman, her husband left in the countryside, Rose a housewife now, with a baby, living in Bexhill, Maisy a secretary in an office. *They are so conventional*, Frances had written to her. *They only want to be normal.*

Ivy tried to hold herself apart from the street as she walked through it: she was *in the world but not of the world*, as Mother Superior would say. And even if she had wanted the world, it had all arrived too late for her, she began to feel. Or she herself was too late. A cool clarity passed over her as she realized this, the particular feeling of *too late* like something lifting from her life, revealing what lay beneath it.

She should walk away, she knew; her life no longer had

space for Frances, for *love*, expressed in such a narrow way, as one single human to another. She should turn back, turn away. The truth struck her, as she watched a little girl holding her nanny's hand, being led along the street: she could not bear that pain ever again.

But here was the house: *24 Alderney Street*. A green door, she saw. She tried to repeat that to herself, calmly. *Green door.* She would know, now, when she read the letters. She could picture Frances sitting at one of the tall, bisected windows that stood over the wide, handsome doorway, watching the busy street pass by. She would know the shops Frances walked by every day, the small square of a park nearby. Ivy had passed the bakery where she must buy her bread, with its peeling red facade. There was the throw of the sky behind the buildings, the expanse of daylight that greeted Frances every fresh day. This would be enough, Ivy told herself. This had to be enough. But there was a face at the window – she tried to turn away – and then quickly, too quickly, a thumping like a child running down stairs, and the green door was open, and here, truly here, was Frances herself.

Ivy? My God.

There was a second of surprise – of separation, of disbelief that Ivy was standing on the grey pavement, wearing a grey habit – but then Frances moved forward, and Ivy moved to meet her. They embraced; there was a sense, for a moment, that the whole street – the whole city – met in their arms, that they held it together. Ivy smelt Frances's neck – somehow unchanged – felt the brush of hair across her nose. Frances kissed her, just briefly, on the cheek: Ivy sensed years returning to her, a whole forgotten existence of feeling. Perhaps, she thought, it had been a mistake, coming here.

They pulled apart: *What are you—? Where did you—?* Frances laughed, gave up on her questions. Ivy for a second felt that they could kiss properly, right there on the doorstep: two women, one of them a nun! But Frances turned around; she led Ivy into the house, through a long, gloomy corridor, and into a kitchen, radiant with sun. It was like the first time she had seen a film in Technicolor, Ivy thought later: this journey from dark to light, the moment when she realized what kind of place Frances lived in.

The kitchen was large and almost formless, a few units scattered around its edges, a round wooden table at its centre. Almost every inch of the wall was covered, as at Cressingdon. But there were no fine paintings: these were posters, dominated by text, large messages that seemed to be shouting with joy or anger: *RISE UP! SMASH THE RICH!* From the ceiling, several wooden racks hung, the colours of the clothes like flags against the pale sun-yellow of the walls. Around the table, five or six people were seated, one bouncing a baby on his knee. They were young, it seemed to Ivy; the men wore tight black jeans: all of them had beards.

I found the pens, Frances said to them. And then: *This is my friend, Ivy—*

She said this in a relaxed, offhand way, as though Ivy's habit were nothing unusual. And in turn the men – and one woman – greeted her with a cool calmness, lifting cigarettes or mugs in greeting, only one raising his eyebrows in surprise.

Sit down, said Frances, *I'll get you some tea. We were just about to start a meeting—*

Frances herself looked different, Ivy saw now, her clothes not dissimilar to what her own daughter Pansy preferred, the long smock in turn like something Marina would wear on a painting day, her hair uncut, rough at the ends. One man cleared his throat.

Right, well, we've got the musicians on board. We just need to—

The baby on his knee gave a loud, indignant yell and was passed to the woman Ivy presumed to be his mother. She lifted a single pale breast from her dress – making no effort to conceal herself – and began to feed him. He gulped hungrily, his legs cycling in the air.

Frances brought Ivy her tea and sat beside her. She reached – as though it was the most simple thing in the world – and held her hand for two seconds, three, before letting go. Ivy felt a moment of shimmering disbelief: she expected the room to break up, to curl into itself like a poster unfurled, to ebb into another morning as a dream. But the meeting continued.

Did Ivan say who would be painting the banner? I thought it could be— Frances's voice had a new authority, a confidence that Ivy recognized not from her own experience but from Joseph's description of her, all those decades ago. *She is so free*, he had said. *So alive.*

Around Frances, people listened; they replied. One of them opened the door to let some air in. Outside, Ivy could smell a meal, smoke, the day settling in to the houses, filling them with expectation. The baby's legs kicked in the sunshine. Somewhere, far away, someone was playing the saxophone, the notes rising into the sky.

I have to go, Ivy told Frances when the meeting was over. *It's Mother*— She had already explained it to Frances, in her last letter. But now the whole plan seemed abstract: she could barely picture Cressingdon, let alone Marina's face.

Of course— Frances paused, picking at a thread on her dress, then looking up fully into Ivy's eyes. *But you will come back – see me again?*

I'm a nun now, Frances – I can't just – I've taken a vow—

As friends, I mean? Frances's eyes were strained.

Ivy paused. *As friends.* She had only been permitted one day's leave, for a dire circumstance. She would not be allowed to simply waltz to London whenever she felt like it. She could just imagine the discussions that would follow with Mother Superior – the readings in discipline, obedience.

Ivy looked up. She shook her head, slowly.

No. It's impossible. I'm – sorry—

Frances bit her lower lip; Ivy could see its colour changing. She put her hand up, as though to stop her.

We can still write letters— Ivy glanced around. The others had dispersed, fading tactfully into other tasks; the chopping of vegetables, the baby swooped away. Frances inhaled deeply.

You could – will you come and see my room?

Ivy looked down. She felt too warm, again, almost suffocated by all that was at her throat, covering her head, the layers and layers against her skin. She should say no, again, though it had been hard enough the first time. She should leave, into the cooling air of the day. She should go to Marina: she should never have come here. But when she looked up Frances was smiling, her voice light.

Just for a minute—?

There was something about her expression – it reminded Ivy, all at once, of the girl she had met so many years ago, walking through the gate at Cressingdon, just when they had given up hope; the way her clothes blended into greenness, so that all they could see was face and hands, those features somehow the answer to the day, the sight that lifted everything.

★

They sat together in Frances's small, pale bedroom, on the edge of her single bed, the daylight a smudged pastel at the window. Like Ivy, it seemed that Frances had been returned to girlhood as an older woman, to single beds with patterned bedspreads, a print tacked on to the wall.

It's nice— Ivy said, and they laughed. Ivy wondered if Frances was thinking, as she was, of the other bedrooms they had stood in together – Ivy's childhood room, her married bedroom where Frances undressed in front of her, all those years ago. Frances's own married room, with its iron bedstead, its wedding photo on the dressing table.

But now Frances lifted her fingers to Ivy's headdress, traced a shape – a perfect oval – around it. Ivy closed her eyes.

Can I take it off? Her voice so quiet.

Ivy shook her head. But then—

Yes— The word seeming to come without intention, almost from her body itself, just as the words of the Psalms now tumbled from her lips without her, as though written across her tongue.

She closed her eyes as Frances's fingers worked over the complicated fastenings, a key in a lock, until she was lifting the covering from Ivy's damp head, the coolness of air moving through Ivy's mind, a tear rolling down her cheek. She had forgotten – so much. How distracting Frances's touch was, the way a simple stroke of her arm would liquefy her thoughts. Frances did not understand this, at first, would think Ivy had simply lost the thread, misplaced what she was saying. But she came to recognize the signs, Ivy's speech stuttering to a halt, her eyes closing, briefly, before opening again with a smile.

Frances took Ivy's face in her hands.

Look at you—

She put her nose against Ivy's. They stayed like that for a few seconds, their breath heavy with the thick, humid life of the moment. Here we are, Ivy kept thinking. *Here we are.*

When Frances kissed her, Ivy felt it: desire, rising again. Such a force, *strong as God*, it seemed to her in that moment. There was no time for guilt. There was only this: the fountain of want, the sheer power of it. It was delirium, and a giving-up: no wonder the Church was so afraid of it. But was there not a purity in it, Ivy thought now, when it was like this? There was nothing of the world.

They took their clothes off, lay on top of the bedspread. Ivy was conscious of her heavy, ancient layers, her standard-issue underwear.

The least erotic garments imaginable— She whispered this to Frances, who in reply kissed her earlobe, her neck, her shoulder, her breast. *Miracle.* This word came to her freely, made her face open wide. There had been days, in the convent, when everything had seemed miraculous to her, when her soul became fast with God. Rain on leaves was miraculous, and the black cows miraculous, like widows massing on the hill. Her own steps were miraculous, and every one of her Sisters. Ivy had walked in a kind of reverie on those days, every step sacred.

Now, she held Frances's arms above her, pressed her against the pillow, so that both of them were stretched, reaching, like angels. She lowered her head, kissed Frances's forehead, a kind of blessing. She forgave Frances, truly now, having no idea forgiveness could feel like this: as though her body were made entirely of light.

Hours later, Ivy walked towards her train, the day beginning to dim around her, a new softness marking each one of her steps. It was almost five: they must be wondering where she was. Anne's baking would be turning stale on the scrubbed kitchen table. The light would be warming the barn, settling across the curves of the statues. Ivy considered, for a brief moment, not boarding the train at all – not seeing Marina – but turning back, to the light of the street, to Frances's house beyond it.

But of course she carried on: to another platform, to the small carriage that would take her almost to Cressingdon, to the station with its tipping sign. To Marina, to Angus, to Anne, who had asked Ivy to pray for them all, in her last letter. She was the one member of the household – the one person in Ivy's former life – who was happy with her vocation. *God needs you*, she had said, pressing her hands over Ivy's. *You are His beloved child.*

Now, Ivy held on to the wooden cross around her neck, thought of Jesus, of the way He walked towards His own death. Should she not pick up her cross? Was every calling not a sacrifice at least as great as this? She could always think of Frances, and surely that was enough. It was such a small thing to give – this real presence, this touch, even the ecstasy itself – when other saints had given so much, had given their very lives.

She reached the train station, where the air was thick with steam and travel, the actions of people convinced there was a purpose to their movements, their continual lifting and carrying, buying and selling, going from one place to another. Soon, Ivy told herself, she would be back in her cell: she would lift her hands to the Lord. He would comfort her. Her life there would continue as it always did, the push and pull of God's presence, a circle like the seasons themselves, the nuns' slow travel through the liturgical year. It was a life of devotion, and what could have more meaning than that? Ivy saw her carriage, the small, careful box of it, its neat rows of seats. She reached for the handle. She did not turn it, but remained, just for a moment, the dying light of the day upon her.

She approached Cressingdon in a taxi, as she had so many times before, feeling shepherded, gentled back to her child-hood home by a man who did not know her, who asked

only the most perfunctory questions before lapsing back into
his own calm silence. The road was hushed, heavily green
already; Ivy wound down the window and smelt what she
knew she would: spring in this place, the same every year,
layers of certain leaves, blossom, the soil itself, sweet and
complicated. Nature did not know that decades had passed
since she had been a girl here, smelling the same thick
draught of place. It only repeated its song: a chorus of apple
blossom, ash leaves, the sap of a birch rising, a glinting gold
beneath its bark.

The taxi rolled into the driveway, the crunch of the
gravel beneath its wheels a particular welcome, the car
facing the anonymous quiet of the front of the house, the
ordinary spacing of windows and doors that gave no clue as
to what was inside. For a moment, all was still. Ivy rum-
maged in her purse for the fare, thinking of how she might
have to knock – to knock! – at the front door, something
she had never done before. But here: it was flung open.
Anne was there, hunched and almost too old to work now,
but her face so remarkably the same, the way it glowed in
the very last of the evening sunshine, every feature seeming
picked out by the light for preference, the glide of her nose,
the rising beams of her cheeks as she smiled at Ivy, opened
her arms.

You're here. Don't you look wonderful—
So sorry I'm late—
The two women pressed together, Ivy's face in the

flour-smell of Anne's shoulder, her breath falling into her apron, the soft relief of it. What was Anne's vocation? Ivy had wondered. Certainly she seemed to love cooking, caring for others, Cressingdon itself, but how often had Ivy seen her almost broken at the end of the day, folded into herself with exhaustion? Did God intend anyone to be a servant? He intended everyone to be a servant, she believed, and thus nobody at all.

Ivy removed her coat, put her small travelling case down. She had not been given – had not even sought – overnight permission, so rarely granted, and not looked on favourably by Mother Superior. She knew it would most likely be as last time, Marina recovering before she even arrived, but the duty remained, the pull to come on command. And she was not, she found, sorry to be here.

Cup of tea, before—?

Ivy nodded; they moved through the hall towards the kitchen, the house with its own scent-map of familiarity.

Pansy – I mean, Peace – is here, and Genevieve. Gilbert is – on his way.

Of course. Ivy had learnt of her daughter's change of name at a Lyon's Corner House almost a year ago. Pansy had been late, as usual: Ivy had sat alone, conspicuous in her habit, the café's furnishings somehow a dull, weathered impersonation of the garden room at Cressingdon, dusky pink upholstery, embroidered cushions. At first, Ivy had not recognized the young woman who half-stumbled towards the table, a cloth bag hitting the back of her legs, clogs or some such heavy shoes making an extraordinary sound on the carpeted floor. Pansy had worn her hair in two long sheets on either side of her scalp, and what looked like a fairy crown, tiny cloth flowers across her forehead.

Mummy! the girl was calling. *I'll never get used to you like that.*

And as though in a dream, the anonymous person had transformed into the known, her features changing into those Ivy had seen at her birth, the perfect, inevitable constellation of eyes, nose and mouth.

Pansy, she had said, getting up to hug her. Pansy smelt of herbs, as though she had been rolling in a kitchen garden, and Ivy thought of Madam Cynthia, all those years ago. *Patchouli*, she knew it was called now. Some of the younger nuns even smelt of it, when they had first arrived.

It's Peace now, her daughter said into her ear, and Ivy had nodded, thinking this was some modern greeting, a version of *shalom*.

Peace now, she'd repeated. But her daughter made a face as she pulled away.

I mean, my name is Peace, now. Not Pansy any more.

There was a particular distancing, Ivy thought now, in your child throwing off the name you gave them at birth, as though they threw off the birth itself, Pansy's own wartime entrance into the world, the sense of urgency echoed in the news surrounding them, the baby like a gift of outrage, her mouth wide open, yelling. But her name had always been a point of confusion: she had become Pansy at the age of sixteen, finally refusing to be Baby, after years of seeming to relish it, twisting in her father's lap as he patted her head distractedly: *How's my Baby?* he would say, and Artemis would curl her lip. Artemis: her brilliant child, a prodigy, almost, and yet she hadn't worked, not once. She had married a clever man instead – a diplomat – and travelled the world with him. Her letters always seemed muted, to Ivy, tamped down, somehow, as though some force were trying to push through the words, to convey some other meaning. But Pansy had reassured her: *She's disgustingly happy, Mummy. God! You've got nothing to worry about.* Artemis would not come today, Ivy knew: she was too far away, living in Cairo this year, with servants of her own. No children yet; she had wondered about this, but never wanted to pry.

As they came into the kitchen Ivy saw that things were different, this time. Genevieve sat, so tiny in her old age, not rising as Ivy came in but simply looking up with a diluted smile, reaching one hand towards her. Pansy – Peace – in another shapeless sack-dress, fell against her, a bundle of fabric and scent, her face wet, her mouth open.

Oh, Mummy – she's so poorly—

Ivy pulled back from Peace and kissed her, once, on her cheek – still, impossibly, the softness of her girlhood. She reached for Genevieve's hand. She recognized – in both of their faces – other illnesses, other deaths. Bear, of course, his death part of her daughter for ever, she knew, like a disease that would never be fully cured. And Hector – just last year, Genevieve seeming to weaken with his death, so that they had all feared she would go with him, as people so often did, as though falling into a hole that has opened beside them.

Marina was not sitting in bed eating toast, Ivy gathered. This was something else. The room flickered, briefly, as though she might faint, or – as it seemed at that moment – the room itself might faint, simply slide away from her, out of view.

Sit for a moment, after your journey, Ivy. Have your tea—

Anne handed her a steaming mug. Ivy found that she wanted Anne beside her, to let herself fall into her bosom – an undignified action for a nun – to cry on her, as Peace had done. But the doorbell was ringing. Her father. Of course he had come, though even later than she had.

Anne bustled away, more laborious than she used to be but still with that same prompt attention. Across the table, Genevieve reached out again, her hands still firm, though impossibly crinkled, the bones just there for Ivy to touch, barely covered. Soon, Ivy thought, her own hands would be this way, just as so many of her Sisters' were. *Too late.* She closed her eyes for a second.

Angus is with her, Genevieve was saying. *We should go up, soon.* Ivy nodded. And here was Gilbert, shambling into the kitchen, elderly and somehow so much the same, as though he had always been elderly, had simply been waiting for the moment to emerge into his true form. He hugged her gingerly, as though afraid, somehow, of her habit.

Ivy, darling. The same automatic affection as always. The same attempt at love.

I'm sorry.

She realized that he was holding her own grief for her, pre-emptively, just as she had held it for her daughters, tried to keep it from them, a monster in a cage. He was still – despite it all – her father. And Marina was still mother, of the same child. There was nothing – no lover, no divorce paper – that could change that, she realized. It was immutable, in a way so little was. It felt of God, in this way.

They sat down at the old kitchen table, every one of its whorls and scratches so familiar, even the sensation of tracing them without looking, a family braille. Gilbert hugged Peace – *so grown up!* – wrapped one arm clumsily around Genevieve.

Would anyone like something to eat with their tea? I've made a pie— Anne gestured to the oven. There was a smell of meat in the air, Ivy realized. It was so familiar, she had almost not noticed, used to the way it bound to the stove, the flowers in their vases, the decorative dishes on the walls. Genevieve and Gilbert shook their heads, frowning slightly, as though the idea was distasteful. But Peace shifted in her seat.

Actually, I'm starving. Could I have some, please, Anne?

Ivy looked at her again: she did seem thinner, her usual round lines sanded down.

Haven't you eaten today, darling?

Peace shook her head. *There's never food in the house really. We don't need much – money's the devil, you know.*

Her face looked defiant now. There was something in the slant of her nose, the force of her eyes; Ivy could see her face at three years old, trying to wrestle a toy from her sister. That particular way her lips pursed into a bud and met her nose. *Doesn't matter!* she used to shout whenever Ivy told her to do something differently. And it always made Ivy stop: Baby was right, she had thought. The spilt milk or ripped dress or ruined toy didn't matter, not truly.

Well, perhaps we can agree there. Ivy sipped her tea. Once Peace had eaten, she would be in a better mood. She always had been grumpy when she was hungry. *How is – Simon?*

He left ages ago. Peace rolled her eyes. *I live with Bobby now. And Nell.*

Ivy nodded calmly, as though this was all to be expected, feeling the others listening, watching. Hadn't her parents had their own complicated arrangements? Gilbert, sitting there, with his string of girlfriends in the past. And she, Ivy, herself? She had thought that the children had known nothing of her and Frances, but there were small comments, over the years, that pointed to some intuition that theirs was not quite an ordinary friendship. When Ivy had first told Artemis about entering the convent, she had frowned and said simply: *But what about Frances?*

Anne lifted the pie from the oven, steaming, a raised impression of a bird on its lid. She cut a slice for Peace, who lowered herself to it immediately with knife and fork, eating as though the food might be stolen at any moment. Genevieve leant forwards to Ivy.

Aren't you hot in all that get-up? They all looked towards her, Anne seeming proud, Gilbert warmly quizzical, as though told a riddle he knew the answer to.

Hmm, it looks boiling, Peace chimed in, her mouth still full of pie. *How's the man upstairs, anyway?* She jabbed with her knife towards the ceiling.

Fine, darling. Ivy smiled, shifted her skirts around. She *was* beginning to feel hot again, too enclosed in the layers of cloth, the woollen stockings. In the past, Ivy had tried to make connections between her life and her daughters'. She had untied ribbons, tried to tie them on to aspects of the way they lived. *Look,* she had said to Peace, *I gave up all worldly goods too. I believe in love and justice, just as you do. Here, Artemis,* she had said, *I do good works in the community. The whole order is dedicated to them.* But the girls had only shrugged, untied the ribbons as quickly and kindly as they could. *Yes, Mother, we know,* they had said, *but it's quite different, you see, for us.*

Now, conversation did not move in its usual ways. Gilbert would not start a theological discussion with her, as he had in the past, and Genevieve would not press her for details of the nunnery – what they ate, whether any of them fell in love with the gardener, or the priest. Genevieve had told her the material could be *gold* for a novel, and yet Ivy always seemed to disappoint her with the mundanity of it all. Or the holiness, the simple dedication of the order, not free from conflict of course but not riddled with it either, not determined by it, and not cursed, in recent years anyway, by any major scandal. But today they would not speak even of this: the afternoon reminded her of wartime, and of early motherhood, these two merged by her own chronology but nonetheless, it seemed to Ivy, sharing an atmosphere, a mode of being. It was crisis: the air prickled with it, turned extraordinary, dailyness thrown into relief, no longer itself but some bygone state of the ordinary, a nostalgia for things still present. Ivy could feel the decades of the house's sameness – in the lines of the windows, the shape of kitchen flagstones – being changed by this day, by these very moments that they sat together, drinking tea.

We should— It was Genevieve who spoke, who reminded them, as though they had forgotten, that Marina was upstairs, that she was, in some sense, waiting.

Perhaps one at a time— Anne said, tentatively. *She gets tired so easily.*

There was a drawing back, a hesitation. Anne looked at the floor, making it clear she would not be the one to decide.

You go, Ivy, Genevieve said. *I've seen her. Pans*— *Peace has seen her, too.*

A hierarchy, then, with Ivy above Gilbert, the fractured union having some consequences, after all. Ivy felt guilty, sickened, almost, that she had lingered so long with Frances, that others had seen Marina before her. That she could have – missed it. But what did Mother Superior say about guilt? It has no purpose unless in confession, and thus transformation. Ivy would make things right: she would go up at once.

But Ivy found she had to stop in the downstairs lavatory first – only installed last year, a tiny, cell-like room. She had to take her headdress off, thinking of Frances's fingers, feeling a dive of desire that made her inhale sharply, even here. But then: the coolness from the small open window on her temples, the hot fabric of her hair swirling across them. She let herself have these seconds: ten, just as at the nunnery, let herself fill with them. She took a breath of the garden air – that unchanged spring. She opened the door.

The ceilings in Marina's bedroom seemed lower than Ivy remembered, dropping into the room as though something was pressing on them from above. Marina was only a shape, at first, a rising of the sheet, the coverlet, a hill of cream. Then a movement, and her hair came into view, the darkness of it, the streaks of silver in the lamplight. Ivy could see that she was even thinner, that her skin itself was thinning, translucent now, as Genevieve's was. Angus rose from his chair at the bedside immediately, more present, somehow, than was usual for him. He dipped Ivy into his arms, as though she was still a young girl, rather than an older woman, and not wearing a habit at all. For the first time since she had arrived Ivy felt a sob well up. Angus was stooping but still graceful, one hand remaining on her shoulder.

Ivy? Is that you? Marina's voice was a swelling croak, a frog in the dusk. Angus let go, and Ivy moved towards the bed.

Oh, good God – you're wearing that.

She was almost relieved, that her mother still had the strength to mock her, to care that she was wearing her habit, her headdress fastened neatly again. She went closer: she was used to being at the bedsides of the sick. So many of her Sisters had died, even since she had been at the convent. It seemed strange, but these deaths had been some of her favourite, most potent moments of her vocation, the sense of God so dense it could not be questioned, rooms so quiet and holy she could hardly breathe within them. Death was only a slipping away, she had felt at those moments. It was not as large as she had imagined.

Hello, Mother. There was the same wooden chair that had always been there: Ivy sat down, arranged the folds of her habit so they lay flat. Her mother had one hand on top of her covers, and Ivy held it: she imagined how her skin felt to Marina, the heat of it, its weight. Ivy was larger than she had ever been: she enjoyed it, the extra heft of her body, its warm rise and fall. But she could see Marina frowning.

What do they – feed you in there, darling? All pies?

A pause, as she gathered her breath.

We grow everything ourselves, Mother. There is only rarely meat – Ivy felt the way the expectation of holiness helped her, in moments like these, distancing her from her own feelings. She could not be angry – so she would not be angry. It could be as simple as that. She saw a water glass beside the bed; she lifted it. *Would you like some?*

Marina shook her head. *I don't want – anything. Tell me – about you. What's it like, in that – place?* Every utterance was broken by a fall into breathlessness, before a brief recovery. Ivy cleared her throat.

It's wonderful. Beautiful. I love it there.

That's – I'm – pleased. Marina's eyes were drooping, already.

Now, Marina quietened into sleep again, but Ivy did not go back downstairs. She walked around, noticing a vase that had been moved on to a table, a section of cupboard that was freshly painted. It must have been Angus – an attempt to cheer Marina up, perhaps. They were sunflowers, their faces dense, like honeycomb, a hundred colours of yellow and orange. On the wall beside the window was a painting Ivy had never seen before. There was a small plaque attached to its chipped wooden frame, one of Marina's, an early work. The painting showed one woman in a long, modest black day-dress, leaning towards a table, as though to serve a drink. Opposite her, another woman reclined, naked, on a low armchair. At first glance, they appeared to be the same person; looking again, Ivy encountered the naked woman first, like a precursor to the clothed, her face unreadable, her body reposed, one arm raised over her head. The clothed woman was smiling, mildly, her legs crossed beneath her. Both were wearing shoes. The naked woman's body appeared neither idealized, to Ivy, nor deliberately counter-ideal: she had a soft stomach, comfortable thighs. She looked like a mother.

Ivy thought of the moments before she put her habit on, when she stood entirely naked in her cell, held in its gradual light. How she felt her nakedness under her cloth, had never lost the capacity to be aware of herself, her own breasts, her waist, her legs under the layers of covering. And she thought of her and Frances, of quiet days in the tiny, sloping cottage, just a mile away, how Ivy would undress her right there in the living room while the girls napped above them. The light on Frances's body, the light that seemed to come *from* her body, to move around its surface, so that Ivy felt she was following its progress with her lips. And she thought of them this afternoon, could see the two of them from above, some-how; like an artwork, she thought, a certain painterly radiance to the scene. Was this not art, of a kind?

From the bed, Ivy heard Marina turning, mumbling in her sleep: she moved towards her; however many times she had nursed her Sisters while they died, she found she was afraid; since Bear, she had not witnessed the death of some-one who did not believe, who was moving into a presumed oblivion, an unending eternity of nothing. Ivy wanted to leave before this happened: she had told Angus she could only stay for a few hours, that that was all that was allowed, that she must be back that night.

She thought again of how she would not be back in time for Compline, her favourite office, the smooth lines of the Sisters swaying in the near-darkness of the chapel. *Keep me as the apple of Thine eye. Hide me under the shadow of Thy wings.* She began to hum the tunes under her breath, to feel their gentle liltings. *Let your servant go in peace.* She was lifted by this music, she knew, held by it, as by the hand of God Himself.

Marina coughed: Ivy moved the glass of water towards her and she opened her eyes, took a sip before lowering her head back to the pillow. It was so familiar, this sense of sitting at Marina's bedside, Anne navigating her childhood shoulders through a dusty bedroom, her mother weak and pale on her pillows.

Ivy?

Yes, Mother. Ivy held her hand again, felt the fragility of every bone.

Do you ever see – Frances – these – days?

Ivy had wondered what Marina knew, if she ever saw or suspected something, all those days she and Frances had brought the children around and then disappeared – into the woods, to a field where the grass was high enough. *Such good friends*, she used to say. *Always together.* Ivy remembered how it felt, to be warm in the summer kitchen, Frances reaching for her hand.

I do, Mother. I saw her today – actually.

Marina turned her head towards Ivy: it looked as though it took tremendous strength, as though she were moving an enormous object. She closed her eyes afterwards, breathed faster with the effort. Ivy had seen this before: in Sister Julian, that gentle woman of love, so strong until the very end, when all the strength had left her suddenly, like a breath given out.

And does she ever speak – of Joseph?

Yes – we talk about him all the time. You know we do.

Marina's breath was slowing again: Ivy thought she might be falling asleep. She pictured the journey ahead of her: the rumble of the taxi over the gravel of the drive, the opening of the country road, the small train and the larger, the convent appearing in the darkness, the glowing of candles at its windows. She felt tired, all of a sudden, the full weight of her fifty years on the earth pushing her down.

What had she been thinking, going to see Frances? The truth was, they had not spoken of Joseph. They had, it seemed, finally surpassed their relations to each other *through* him, the sense that he formed a third party between them. But this was one of Marina's greatest fears: that they would forget Joseph. That he would be, in some way, erased, even in memory.

There's something—

Marina closed her eyes again. Her hand fluttered on the bedclothes.

That night. Easter. Every word was an obstacle, an accomplishment.

Why could you not – just drag him to – the bank? It must have been – so close.

Ivy could feel her habit becoming solid around her face, her body. It was much too tight, suddenly, the coif a taut strap around her neck.

I told you, Mother. He was—

And you were such. A good. Swimmer.

Ivy did not want to repeat the story again. She could not: her wimple was pressing her throat. She reached up for a button to loosen it, thinking again of how tender Frances's fingers were, as though undressing a baby. How the whole headpiece had lain before them, like a shed skin.

I tried, Mother.

This was all she could say, she found, and it seemed to be enough. She thought of the way she had sat by the riverbank after Joseph disappeared, shaking so hard her teeth made a sound as they banged together, a horrible music she would hear again and again in her dreams. She had not moved, for many minutes: she had not yelled for help. And then: those still afternoons of mystery, when she had sat in the wet brightness of the studio and it had seemed that there was hope: that Joseph would have survived, like a watery phoenix rising intact from the waters, smiling his Sunday smile. Even after the search was called off, Ivy still felt that he would walk in and put his big hand on the top of her head, like he used to. *No hard feelings, Ive*, he might say. Give her a gentle punch on the shoulder. And her whole vocation: a search for life beginning anew, in some way. For resurrection.

Marina closed her eyes again: she reached for Ivy's hand. Her breathing was slowing still more, her face acquiring a translucent shine. She glanced around for Angus: was this it? It couldn't be, surely. Not yet. Angus came closer, took Marina's other hand. How similar death was to birth, Ivy thought now. This atmosphere, the world opening, God pressing in. It seemed so unlikely, somehow, that this was the moment itself – it had come so fast – though she had heard, many times, of people who waited until a particular loved one arrived before letting go, as though death were entirely in their control. Ivy found it hard to believe that she was the one Marina had waited for, but perhaps – she was her only remaining child, after all. *She has lost her son.* A memory of a voice, decades old. Ivy stood up.

Should I—?

Angus looked haggard, fearful, as diminished as she had ever seen him. He nodded.

Ivy went to the top of the stairs and called out, as she hadn't since she was a girl – these same stairs, witness to so many callings—

Anne! Father! Genevieve!

They came quickly, as though they had been waiting to be called, all of them grouped around the bed now, a look of brotherly tenderness on Gilbert's face, Genevieve folded against him. Ivy put an arm around Peace, who cried softly. Marina's breath was rasping now, like something dragged over a rough surface, impossibly slow. Ivy began to pray the prayer of St Francis, feeling a plain of silence open up before her, a fountain of presence.

Lord, make me an instrument of your peace: where there is hatred, let me sow love—

She thought again of the convent, of the beautiful deaths she had witnessed. The weeks of preparation, of prayer so dense it filled the whole building, so that from the moment she woke up she could taste the holy spirit, present in the fabric of her clothes, the kettle, the sliver of soap she held in the bath. The way she sat with her Sisters around every bed, the sense of God so certain she would not have been surprised to see a body lift from the sheets and ascend to the sky.

—where there is injury, pardon; where there is doubt, faith; where there is despair, hope; where there is darkness, light—

Marina's mouth relaxed, at last: a slant of serenity fell over her features, a look Ivy had never seen. She thought of all the ways she had seen her mother: in silent, concentrated joy, painting with Angus, and in rage, lifting a plate over her head, smashing it to the ground. She saw, for the briefest moment, her mother's young face leaning over her crib, bleached with happiness, her arms reaching in to lift her.

It was raining, as they stood outside together, smoking in the darkness. Nobody talked of umbrellas, nobody fetched a raincoat. How small rain was, compared to what they had witnessed, the way a person could leave the world, leave their lives, and the beds, chairs and tables would stand around as though nothing had happened. Angus was still with Marina: he said he would stay until the doctor arrived, the men from the funeral home in the nearest town, always on guard for death.

Ivy stood between Genevieve and Peace; she refused a cigarette at first, could not quite bear for them to see her smoking in her habit, for this plainly comic image to exist so close to Marina's death. But then she wanted it too much: the deep inhalation, the breath powered by smoke, flowing out of her. She felt that she was supporting the small, thin bodies of her aunt and daughter, fragile in their youth and old age, her middle years a strength between them.

Gilbert looked lost, standing across from them, partly under the cover of a large tree. He smoked one cigarette after another; he beckoned for them to join him. But Ivy was so cooled and refreshed by the rain; she felt she would always like to walk in a gentle rain of this kind, so that her habit never felt too hot or restrictive. In this way, she thought, she could bear it.

On the train water formed stars on the windowpane, whole galaxies of brightness that bent and lurched with the turns of the track. They swayed a little and came to a stop; other passengers shifted around her, but Ivy only felt a smooth, endless patience. The convent was waiting for her, she knew: she would not be back by Compline, but someone would be staying up to release the bolt on the great wooden front door, just for her. One of the younger ones, Sister Vincent, perhaps, stifling her yawns with her sleeve, her head bobbing into sleep before lifting again over her knitting. The paintings in the hallways would be still in the darkness, a cobalt solemnity settling over them all. Religious scenes, only: the Virgin Mary and Mary Magdalene draped over Jesus's bloodied body, their mouths holes of pain, the sleek rivers of their clothes running over him.

The train started up again. Ivy thought of the painting at Cressingdon again, of the two women, one naked, the other clothed: had she not been two women, all her life? Ivy the dreamer, then the nun – and Ivy who lived in the world of objects, was surrounded by it. But, she thought then, was she not naked with God, and with Frances? Did both not love her, and see her as she was? *Let yourself be loved, just as you are*, Anne had said to her, before she made her last profession to the convent. *I have called you by name, you are mine*, Anne quoted. She was thinking of the offices, no doubt, of Ivy's waking in her small cell to the breath of God, falling asleep with Him hovering around her, as an angel. She was not thinking of Frances's hands, the delicacy of them, their softness on her hands and neck, on her stomach and thighs. But Ivy did.

They had arrived, the lights of Victoria station a dance beyond the window. Ivy stepped off the train, began to walk towards the Underground, unable to imagine walking all the way this time. Over her legs, the fabric of her habit fell and gathered, her sensible shoes making their loud sound on the smooth floor, just as they did in the cloister. She was almost at the Underground steps when she saw the exit, the cool gap of its arch, the lights of the city framed within it, Frances's house, she knew, just minutes beyond. She turned, letting herself move like a fish through clear water, her feet no longer sore, her head free from thought. She felt the newly familiar streets around her, people heading home for the night, smells of smoke and onions in the air. *Just as I am*, she thought, as she saw Frances's green door take shape ahead of her. She stood against it for a second before she rang the bell.

Whatever happened in her life from now on, Ivy would always have this moment: the cool air of the city around her, waiting for something she resisted imagining, did not want to give shape in her mind before it took its own reality. There was one small, faltering moment when she thought Frances might not come to the door. That it would be someone else, a near-stranger, and that her journey would continue, after all, into the night, back to the solace of God.

But here, here: she would have endured everything else for this one instant, Frances's face wide, arms around her, voice calling out her name—

Ivy!

DAY SIX

Easter Sunday 1999

FROM HER BEDROOM window, Ivy can see heaven. It changes from day to night, becoming smoky in the evenings, long grey creatures that hang in the air, soft bellies trailing down. She thinks of the smog that used to rest on London like a second city: a place of ghouls and monsters, Ivy thought on visits as a child. But the sky from this window is clear: it is orange and soft now, in the morning. She could lift from the bed and drift into it, she realizes, lie on a cloud and float away.

But the noise: so many cars, just an endless stream. She feels, more than ever, that she is out of time, has outlived her time, now unmoored in this world of gadgets and computers, information only a touch away, on machines she can never begin to understand, however much her grandchildren try to explain them.

Just a setback, the doctor said the last time he came. *You could still have years ahead*—

But Ivy does not think of the future, now. She is only here, in the present, or the long, stretching country of the past. She thinks of certain days – Easter Sunday, in particular – over and over again, feeling her way along its hours like rooms she has lived in. She has learnt that she can occupy a day again, if she pleases, can move within it slowly, its walls sticky with time. She knows that certain images rise, floating, above the others. As she remembers, she marvels: at heaven from the window, at her whole laughable existence. Most of all: at the way a single day can unravel everything, like ribbon pulled from a present, the way it all opened in an instant.

The Easter the year before Joseph died: that long lunch in the garden, Ivy's feet slipping out of her sandals, letting the grass tickle her soles. Bear, in a bright blue shirt, lifting a glass of pale wine to his lips, leaning back to laugh, a warm stream of sound. There was Marina, most of her meal left on her plate, her hair tied loosely, her fingers tapping on her chair. She wanted to paint, Ivy thinks now, and Angus was in the studio already, his plate finished, his chair pushed back.

At the centre of the table: Joseph, flanked by Genevieve and Gilbert, finishing his second portion of lamb, cooked perfectly that day, soft in their mouths. Joseph, in his second year at Oxford, his skin not yet dulled by the fatigue and stubble that would arrive in the summer. He was shining, awake, telling a joke and thumping the table with his hand, so that even Ivy's plate, at the other end, jumped with his force. The trees waved dreamily: they settled into the afternoon, the smell of the air that sweet glide of spring. The hillsides called to them to walk, to move their bodies, as was traditional after lunch, to feel real air in their hearts. But for just a little longer, they sat together. For just a moment, they were quiet.

Now, Ivy heard the creak of the stairs, their familiar, rising music. Frances, advanced in age herself, older than Ivy and yet still caring for her, still bringing her tea at eleven, with a rich tea biscuit propped on the saucer. The door swung open and there she was: still a surprise, somehow, in the cardigan she'd had for thirty years: the brown wool, the deep pockets. Her smile.

Your tea, madam—

It was like the feeling of magic as a child, discovering that life still had bounty, those sunlit days of love in middle age, as she and Frances marched and chanted in all those protests, often with a grandchild on their shoulders. All those years of life together. Who would have known it? She certainly had not, had believed herself to be content with the long, clear life of a nun, dissolving into God with her Sisters at her side. But there was another plan for her, she came to see. Or at least another path. They had even had a ceremony, of a kind, a soaring afternoon by the river, one of their friends the officiate, Artemis reading a poem, even one of Ivy's old Sisters watching, another who had left the nunnery. They would love each other for ever, she and Frances said that day. And they had.

Would you like your book?

Frances motioned to a pile of novels on the bedside table, her reading glasses propped against them. Ivy shook her head, smiling.

I'm just – thinking today.

Frances looked at her for a moment, lifted one of her hands: she kissed it.

Happy Easter. They looked out of the window, at the sky, still streaked with pink. *I'm trying to roast a chicken for us, not sure how it will turn out – we'll see—*

Frances left after a few minutes, calling as she went to see if Ivy would prefer carrots or peas, pulling the door closed behind her. She liked to play loud music in the kitchen; she was a terrible cook. But she tried. Anne had passed on her old cookbook to them, before she died, but they had given it back to Cressingdon. A museum now, of a kind, where people visited, where they bought gifts for their mothers, mugs and tea towels covered with Marina's work. Angus had collapsed in the studio, in front of a canvas, a brush in his hand, not long after Marina died. *It was perfect*, people said. *Just what he would have wanted.* Ivy had returned to Cressingdon soon afterwards, was amazed at how each room kept history complete, static: days, weeks, hours and seconds of her life, all there, in its walls, its floors, each and every painting. People adored the place, she was told: they claimed it for their own.

★

Easter morning when she was a young child, perhaps four or five: curled on Marina's lap, the rise of her mother's breast under her cheek, the smell of her sweat in Ivy's mouth. Marina was talking to Angus, who was frying eggs on the stove, and the birds were dancing in the trees outside the window, jumping from branch to branch.

An Easter as an older child: ten, perhaps eleven. She was sitting under the table, though Joseph teased her for it, having a tea party for the ladybirds: daisy-head cups, a drop of water against their wings. She was feeling strange, that day: there had been a mustiness around her mind from the moment she woke, swords in her throat that made her unable to eat. She hadn't wanted to miss the party, but now she was so hot the under-table world began to tip and unbalance, the adults' shoes rising to meet her.

Scarlet fever, they said later: she was carried to bed by Angus, felt his arms swoop under her body like the wing of an enormous bird. *A swan*, she had thought, as she lay there, feeling herself softly levitating from the mattress, one inch, then two. Everything was large: her skull and her nose and her hands, which puffed and floated in front of her face. She imagined that she could swell and fill the whole room, that she would fill the house. People moved in and out, a doctor came and went, the sun rose and set; it danced, she imagined, teasing her. Anne came, with broth and flannels, with an orange cut into gleaming slices, like jewels. Once, Marina was there, in her home-made dress, her hair tucked behind her ears. Her smell: paint water, lemons. And she was gone.

Three years before Joseph died: they had lain in the garden for most of the day, it was so warm. Ivy had felt like a cat herself, stretched and languorous on an Indian bedspread. She was reading *The Tempest*, feeling the futility of trying to write at all, if she could not be Shakespeare. It was her *latest craze*, as Marina put it.

Scribbling in that notebook – like Bear! Like Genevieve! I thought you would be an ignorant artist, one of us—

The Easter Joseph died. Ivy had seen him and Marina in the garden room that afternoon, once the lamb was eaten, its smell still lowering through the house. It was before coffee: she remembered the shadow they had made on the rug, the way its leaves and diamonds were darkened by their shapes. Marina, reaching to his face, inspecting his broken tooth, perhaps, but then her fingers holding his cheeks: such gentleness in her touch, Ivy could tell, even from where she stood. She could not remember the last time her mother had touched her in that way. Had even looked at her in the way she was looking at Joseph: with naked, uncomprehending love.

★

That same Easter, in the morning, walking in from the garden: Joseph was swinging his arms, jubilant. *I really do like her, Ivy*, she remembered him saying, lifting a twig, snapping it in two. *I think I might ask her to marry me.* And Ivy had laughed and chased him with a handful of soil, calling: *Husband! Husband!*

Ivy could still see the wedding of Frances and Joseph, as she had imagined it that day, before she had even met Frances. She had seen a gilded woman, radiant with beauty, walking with Joseph to the light. Sometimes, she imagined happiness as a golden ball, an object that she had wrestled from Joseph, taken for her own.

Later that day, she saw them – Frances and Joseph – while Anne was making cocoa, Marina busying herself elsewhere. They were alone, in the drawing room, two figures against the window, Frances much shorter, Joseph with his fingers curled around her chin. He was lifting her face to his, and they were kissing, not a short kiss but one that lengthened and spread, until Frances's hands were in his hair, his fingers down the length of her body, pulling her closer and closer. Ivy had stood at the bottom of the stairs and watched them, for as long as she could: she soaked the kiss into her. She made it part of her life.

★

That night in the water: wasn't there, if she thinks carefully enough, if she pushes until it hurts, wasn't there a moment when she could have saved him? When he called to her. She thinks of it now, she makes herself: the black water, his voice, wet, choking.

Ivy.

But she had kept her face fixed on the light, on mystery, the mystery that would pull her, like an engine, for the rest of her life. She had chosen.

Ivy closes her eyes: she sees now, more clearly than she ever has, that all time exists at once, no beginning or end to it. *The eternal now*, Mother Superior used to say. *Eternity is right here with us.* Now, still, though no longer a nun, Ivy can feel God so close: just at her elbow. How much she is forgiven, she knows: how much they are all forgiven, in the end.

Her life flows around her, it lifts: the night Joseph died, the funeral, watching from the roof during the war, sitting in that small bedroom so many years later, a tear rolling down her cheek. It falls: a gramophone. A chapel. A shining hallway. A pie with a bird. Her daughters: their faces at birth. Bear. Marina. Gilbert. Genevieve. Angus. Anne.

And Frances, and Frances, and Frances – in so many moments, so many gifts of happiness. Ivy feels it all gather, gather, a wash of life, of grace and welcome. There is light, as mysterious as that which she glimpsed overhead, so many decades ago, still unknown to her. And there is love, above all: that which she saw in the darkness, and at the height of the sky. She moves towards it. She does not stop.

Acknowledgments

This novel took various forms over the years. My heartfelt thanks to all those who helped to guide it into being through readings and conversation, including Kaddy Benyon, Rebecca Birrell, Tamsin Palmer, Rebecca Sollom and Richard Springer.

Deep gratitude as always to my agent, Emma Paterson, and to my editors Sophie Jonathan and Elisabeth Schmitz. Many thanks to Camilla Elworthy, Laura Schmitt, Daisy Dickeson, Laura Carr and all at Picador, Grove Atlantic, C. H. Beck and my publishers around the world. Thank you to the staff of St Beuno's, Charleston, Hughes Hall and Cambridge University Library, and to the Royal Literary Fund for their support.

Finally, to my family and friends, for their love and encouragement. To every single one of you, and in memory of Anthea Morrison. Thank you for giving me so many days of light.

A Note on Sources

Although all characters in the novel are fictional, a wide range of books and other sources inspired its writing. Many of these focus on Charleston in Sussex and its inhabitants, including *Selected Letters of Vanessa Bell* edited by Regina Marler (Bloomsbury, 1993), *Bloomsbury's Outsider: A Life of David Garnett* by Sarah Knights (Bloomsbury Reader, 2015), and particularly *Deceived with Kindness* by Angelica Garnett (Pimlico, 1993) and *Vanessa Bell* by Frances Spalding (Weidenfeld & Nicolson, 1983).

The scene in which Marina quotes Bear's words at Ivy's birth was inspired by a letter from David Garnett to Lytton Strachey quoted in *Vanessa Bell* (p. 177). The painting described on pp. 249–50 is based on *Interior with Two Women* by Vanessa Bell (1932).

The advice on gas masks for children was produced by the Ministry of Home Security and can be found at the National Archives: https://www.nationalarchives.gov.uk/education/resources/home-front/source-3c/

The book Ivy reads on Day Three is *The Practice of the*

Presence of God and Spiritual Maxims by Brother Lawrence, trans. Donald Attwater (Incense House Publishing, 2013, first published 1692).